THE
TERRIBLE TWINS

EDGAR JEPSON

1st WORLD
LIBRARY
Literary Society

The Terrible Twins

Edgar Jepson

© 1st World Library, 2007
PO Box 2211
Fairfield, IA 52556
www.1stworldlibrary.com
First Edition

LCCN: 2007927781

Softcover ISBN: 978-1-4218-4527-2
Hardcover ISBN: 978-1-4218-4443-5
eBook ISBN: 978-1-4218-4611-8

Purchase *"The Terrible Twins"*
as a traditional bound book at:
www.1stWorldLibrary.com/purchase.asp?ISBN=978-1-4218-4527-2

1st World Library is a literary, educational organization
dedicated to:

- Creating a free internet library of downloadable ebooks

- Hosting writing competitions and offering book publishing
  scholarships.

Interested in more 1st World Library books? contact:
literacy@1stworldlibrary.com
Check us out at: www.1stworldlibrary.com

1st World Library Literary Society

Giving Back to the World

"If you want to work on the core problem, it's early school literacy."

- James Barksdale, former CEO of Netscape

"No skill is more crucial to the future of a child, or to a democratic and prosperous society, than literacy."

- Los Angeles Times

"Literacy... means far more than learning how to read and write... The aim is to transmit... knowledge and promote social participation."

- UNESCO

"Literacy is not a luxury, it is a right and a responsibility. If our world is to meet the challenges of the twenty-first century we must harness the energy and creativity of all our citizens."

- President Bill Clinton

"Parents should be encouraged to read to their children, and teachers should be equipped with all available techniques for teaching literacy, so the varying needs and capacities of individual kids can be taken into account."

- Hugh Mackay

CONTENTS

CHAPTER I

AND CAPTAIN BASTER

For all that their voices rang high and hot, the Twins were really discussing the question who had hit Stubb's bull-terrier with the greatest number of stones, in the most amicable spirit. It was indeed a nice question and hard to decide since both of them could throw stones quicker, straighter and harder than any one of their size and weight for miles and miles round; and they had thrown some fifty at the bull-terrier before they had convinced that dense, but irritated, quadruped that his master's interests did not really demand his presence in the orchard; and of these some thirty had hit him. Violet Anastasia Dangerfield, who always took the most favorable view of her experience, claimed twenty hits out of a possible thirty; Hyacinth Wolfram Dangerfield, in a very proper spirit, had at once claimed the same number; and both of them were defending their claims with loud vehemence, because if you were not loudly vehement, your claim lapsed.

Suddenly Hyacinth Wolfram, as usual, closed the discussion; he said firmly, "I tell you what: we both hit that dog the same number of times."

So saying, he swung round the rude calico bag, bulging with

booty, which hung from his shoulders, and took from it two Ribston pippins.

"Perhaps we did," said Anastasia amiably. They went swiftly down the road, munching in a peaceful silence.

It had been an odd whim of nature to make the Twins so utterly unlike. No stranger ever took Violet Anastasia Dangerfield, so dark-eyed, dark-haired, dark-skinned, of so rich a coloring, so changeful and piquant a face, for the cousin, much less for the twin-sister, of Hyacinth Wolfram Dangerfield, so fair-skinned, fair-haired, blue-eyed, on whose firmly chiseled features rested so perpetual, so contrasting a serenity. But it was a whim of man, of their wicked uncle Sir Maurice Falconer, that had robbed them of their pretty

[Transcriber's note: page 3 missing]

[Transcriber's note: page 4 missing]

demand, had forbidden them to use them any longer.

The Twins always obeyed their mother; but they resented bitterly the action of Little Deeping. It was, indeed, an ungrateful place, since their exploits afforded its old ladies much of the carping conversation they loved. In a bitter and vindictive spirit the Twins set themselves to become the finest stone-throwers who ever graced a countryside; and since they had every natural aptitude in the way of muscle and keenness of eye, they were well on their way to realize their ambition. There may, indeed, have been northern boys of thirteen who could outthrow the Terror, but not a girl in England could throw a stone straighter or harder than Erebus.

Edgar Jepson

They came to a gate opening on to Little Deeping common; Erebus vaulted it gracefully; the Terror, hampered by the bag of booty, climbed over it (for the Twins it was always simpler to vault or climb over a gate than to unlatch it and walk through) and took their way along a narrow path through the gorse and bracken. They had gone some fifty yards, when from among the bracken on their right a voice cried: "Bang-g-g! Bang-g-g!"

The Twins fell to the earth and lay still; and Wiggins came out of the gorse, his wooden rifle on his shoulder, a smile of proud triumph on his richly freckled face. He stood over the fallen Twins; and his smile of triumph changed to a scowl of fiendish ferocity.

"Ha! Ha! Shot through the heads!" he cried. "Their bones will bleach in the pathless forest while their scalps hang in the wigwam of Red Bear the terror of the Cherokees!"

Then he scalped the Twins with a formidable but wooden knife. Then he took from his knickerbockers pocket a tattered and dirty note-book, an inconceivable note-book (it was the only thing to curb the exuberant imagination of Erebus) made an entry in it, and said in a tone of lively satisfaction: "You're only one game ahead."

"I thought we were three," said Erebus, rising.

"They're down in the book," said Wiggins; firmly; and his bright blue eyes were very stern.

"Well, we shall have to spend a whole afternoon getting well ahead of you again," said Erebus, shaking out her dark curls.

Wiggins waged a deadly war with the Twins. He ambushed and scalped them; they ambushed and scalped him. Seeing that they had already passed their thirteenth birthday, it was a great condescension on their part to play with a boy of ten; and they felt it. But Wiggins was a favored friend; and the game filled intervals between sterner deeds.

The Terror handed Wiggins an apple; and the three of them moved swiftly on across the common. Wiggins was one of those who spurn the earth. Now and again, for obscure but profound reasons, he would suddenly spring into the air and proceed by leaps and bounds.

Once when he slowed down to let them overtake him, he said, "The game isn't really fair; you're two to one."

"You keep very level," said the Terror politely.

"Yes; it's my superior astuteness," said Wiggins sedately.

"Goodness! What words you use!" said Erebus in a somewhat jealous tone.

"It's being so much with my father; you see, he has a European reputation," Wiggins explained.

"Yes, everybody says that. But what is a European reputation?" said Erebus in a captious tone.

"Everybody in Europe knows him," said Wiggins; and he spurned the earth.

They called him Wiggins because his name was Rupert. It seemed to them a name both affected and ostentatious. Besides, crop it as you might, his hair *would* assume the appearance of a mop.

They came out of the narrow path into a broader rutted

Edgar Jepson

cart-track to see two figures coming toward them, eighty yards away.

"It's Mum," said Erebus.

Quick as thought the Terror dropped behind her, slipped off the bag of booty, and thrust it into a gorse-bush.

"And—and—it's the Cruncher with her!" cried Erebus in a tone in which disgust outrang surprise.

"Of all the sickening things! The Cruncher!" cried the Terror, echoing her disgust. "What's he come down again for?"

They paused; then went on their way with gloomy faces to meet the approaching pair.

The gentleman whom they called the "Cruncher," and who from their tones of disgust had so plainly failed to win their young hearts was Captain Baster of the Twenty-fourth Hussars; and they called him the Cruncher on account of the vigor with which he plied his large, white, prominent teeth.

They had not gone five yards when Wiggins said in a tone of superiority: "*I* know why he's come down."

"Why?" said the Terror quickly.

"He's come down to marry your mother," said Wiggins.

"What?" cried the Twins with one voice, one look of blank consternation; and they stopped short.

"How dare you say a silly thing like that?" cried Erebus fiercely.

"*I* didn't say it," protested Wiggins. "Mrs. Blenkinsop said it."

"That silly old gossip!" cried Erebus.

"And Mrs. Morton said it, too," said Wiggins. "They came to tea yesterday and talked about it. I was there: there was a plum cake—one of those rich ones from Springer's at Rowington. And they said it would be such a good thing for both of you because he's so awfully rich: the Terror would go to Eton; and you'd go to a good school and get a proper bringing-up and grow up a lady, after all—"

"I wouldn't go! I should hate it!" cried Erebus.

"Yes; they said you wouldn't like wholesome discipline," said the faithful reporter. "And they didn't seem to think your mother would like it either—marrying the Cruncher."

"Like it? She wouldn't dream of it—a bounder like that!" said the Terror.

"I don't know—I don't know—if she thought it would be good for us—she'd do anything for us—you know she would!" cried Erebus, wringing her hands in anxious fear.

The Terror thrust his hands into his pockets; his square chin stuck out in dogged resolution; a deep frown furrowed his brow; and his face was flushed.

"This must be stopped," he said through his set teeth.

"But how?" said Erebus.

"We'll find a way. It's war!" said the Terror darkly.

Wiggins spurned the earth joyfully: "I'm on your side," he said. "I'm a trusty ally. He called me Freckles."

"Come on," said the Terror. "We'd better face him."

They walked firmly to meet the detested enemy. As they drew near, the Terror's face recovered its flawless serenity; but Erebus was scowling still.

From twenty yards away Captain Baster greeted them in a rich hearty voice: "How's Terebus and the Error; and how's Freckles?" he cried, and laughed heartily at his own delightful humor.

The Twins greeted him with a cold, almost murderous politeness; Wiggins shook hands with Mrs. Dangerfield very warmly and left out Captain Baster.

"I'm always pleased to see you with the Twins, Wiggins," said Mrs. Dangerfield with her delightful smile. "I know you keep them out of mischief."

"It's generally all over before I come," said Wiggins somewhat glumly; and of a sudden it occurred to him to spurn the earth.

"I've not had that kiss yet, Terebus. I'm going to have it this time I'm here," said Captain Baster playfully; and he laughed his rich laugh.

"Are you?" said Erebus through her clenched teeth; and she gazed at him with the eyes of hate.

They turned; and Mrs. Dangerfield said, "You'll come to tea with us, Wiggins?"

"Thank you very much," said Wiggins; and he spurned the earth. As he alighted on it once more, he added. "Tea at other people's houses is so much nicer than at home. Don't you think so, Terror?"

"I always eat more—somehow," said the Terror with a grave smile.

They walked slowly across the common, a protecting twin on either side of Mrs. Dangerfield; and Captain Baster, in the strong facetious vein, enlivened the walk with his delightful humor. The gallant officer was the very climax of the florid, a stout, high-colored, black-eyed, glossy-haired young man of twenty-eight, with a large tip-tilted nose, neatly rounded off in a little knob forever shiny. The son of the famous pickle millionaire, he had enjoyed every advantage which great wealth can bestow, and was now enjoying heartily a brave career in a crack regiment. The crack regiment, cold, phlegmatic, unappreciative, was not enjoying it. To his brother officers he was known as Pallybaster, a name he had won for himself by his frequent remark, "I'm a very pally man." It was very true: it was difficult, indeed, for any one whom he thought might be useful to him, to avoid his friendship, for, in addition to all the advantages which great wealth bestows, he enjoyed an uncommonly thick skin, an armor-plate impenetrable to snubs.

All the way to Colet House, he maintained a gay facetious flow of personal talk that made Erebus grind her teeth, now and again suffused the face of Wiggins with a flush of mortification that dimmed his freckles, and wrinkled Mrs. Dangerfield's white brow in a distressful frown. The Terror, serene, impassive, showed no sign of hearing him; his mind was hard at work on this very serious problem with which he had been so suddenly confronted. More than once Erebus countered a witticism with a sharp retort, but with none sharp enough to pierce the rhinocerine hide of the gallant officer. Once this unbidden but humorous guest was under their roof, the laws of hospitality denied her even this relief. She could only treat him with a steely civility. The steeliness did not check the easy flow of his wit.

He looked oddly out of his place in the drawing-room of Colet House; he was too new for it. The old, worn, faded, carefully polished furniture, for the most part of the late eighteenth or early nineteenth century, seemed abashed in the presence of his floridness. It seemed to demand the setting of spacious, ornately glittering hotels. Mrs. Dangerfield liked him less in her own drawing-room than anywhere. When her eyes rested on him in it, she was troubled by a curious feeling that only by some marvelous intervention of providence had he escaped calling in a bright plaid satin tie.

The fact that he was not in his proper frame, though he was not unconscious of it, did not trouble Captain Baster. Indeed, he took some credit to himself for being so little contemptuous of the shabby furniture. In a high good humor he went on shining and shining all through tea; and though at the end of it his luster was for a while dimmed by the discovery that he had left his cigarette-case at the inn and there were no cigarettes in the house, he was presently shining again. Then the Twins and Wiggins rose and retired firmly into the garden.

They came out into the calm autumn evening with their souls seething.

"He's a pig—and a beast! We can't let Mum marry him! We *must* stop it!" cried Erebus.

"It's all very well to say 'must.' But you know what Mum is:

if she thinks a thing is for our good, do it she will," said the Terror gloomily.

"And she never consults us—never!" cried Erebus.

"Only when she's a bit doubtful," said the Terror.

"Then she's not doubtful now. She hasn't said a word to us about it," said Erebus.

"That's what looks so bad. It looks as if she'd made up her mind already; and if she has, it's no use talking to her," said the Terror yet more gloomily.

They were silent; and the bright eyes of Wiggins moved expectantly backward and forward from one to the other. He preserved a decorous sympathetic silence.

"No, it's no good talking to Mum," said Erebus presently in a despairing tone.

"Well, we must leave her out of it and just squash the Cruncher ourselves," said the Terror.

"But you can't squash the Cruncher!" cried Erebus.

"Why not? We've squashed other people, haven't we?" said the Terror sharply.

"Never any one so thick-skinned as him," said Erebus.

The Terror frowned deeply again: "We can always try," he said coldly. "And look here: I've been thinking all tea-time: if stepchildren don't like stepfathers, there's no reason why stepfathers should like stepchildren."

"The Cruncher likes us, though it's no fault of ours," said Erebus.

"That's just it; he doesn't really know us. If he saw the kind of stepchildren he was in for, it might choke him off," said the Terror.

"But he can't even see we hate him," objected Erebus.

"No, and if he did, he wouldn't mind, he'd think it a joke. My idea isn't to show him how we feel, but to show him what we can do, if we give our minds to it," said the Terror in a somewhat sinister tone.

Erebus gazed at him, taking in his meaning. Then a dazzling smile illumined her charming face; and she cried: "Oh, yes! Let's give him socks! Let's begin at once!"

"Yes: I'll help! I'm a trusty ally!" cried Wiggins; and he spurned the earth joyfully at the thought.

They were silent a while, their faces grave and intent, cudgeling their brains for some signal exploit with which to open hostilities.

Presently Wiggins said: "You might make him an apple-pie bed. They're very annoying when you're sleepy."

He spoke with an air of experience.

"What's an apple-pie bed?" said Erebus scornfully.

Wiggins hung his head, abashed.

"It's a beginning, anyhow," said the Terror in an approving tone; and he added with the air of a philosopher: "Little things, and big things, they all count."

"I was trying to think how to break his leg; but I can't," said Erebus bitterly.

"By Jove! That cigarette-case! Come on!" cried the Terror; and he led the way swiftly out of the garden and took the path to Little Deeping.

"Where are we going?" said Erebus.

"We're going to make him that apple-pie bed. There's nothing like making a beginning. We shall think of heaps of other things. If we don't worry about them, they'll occur to us. They always do," said the Terror, at once practical and philosophical.

They walked briskly down to The Plough, the one inn of Little Deeping, where, as usual, Captain Baster was staying, and went in through the front door which stood open. At the sound of their footsteps in her hall the stout but good-humored landlady came bustling out of the bar to learn what they wanted.

"Good afternoon, Mrs. Pittaway," said the Terror politely. "We've come for Captain Baster's cigarette-case. He's left it somewhere in his room."

At the thought of handling the shining cigarette-case Mrs. Pittaway rubbed her hands on her apron; then the look of favor with which her eyes had rested on the fair guileless face of the Terror, changed to a frown; and she said: "Bother the thing! It's sure to be stuck somewhere out of sight. And the bar full, too."

"Don't you trouble; I'll get it. I know the bedroom," said the

Terror with ready amiability; and he started to mount the stairs.

"Oh, thank you, sir," said Mrs. Pittaway, bustling back to the bar.

Erebus and Wiggins dashed lightly up the stairs after the Terror. In less than two minutes the deft hands of the Twins had dealt with the bed; and their intelligent eyes were eagerly scanning the hapless unprotected bedroom. Erebus sprang to the shaving-brush on the mantelpiece and thrust it under the mattress. The Terror locked Captain Baster's portmanteau; and as he placed the keys beside the shaving-brush, he said coldly:

"That'll teach him not to be so careless."

Erebus giggled; then she took the water-jug and filled one of Captain Baster's inviting dress-boots with water. Wiggins rocked with laughter.

"Don't stand giggling there! Why don't you do something?" said Erebus sharply.

Wiggins looked thoughtful; then he said: "A clothes-brush in bed is very annoying when you stick your foot against it."

He stepped toward the dressing-table; but the Terror was before him. He took the clothes-brush and set it firmly, bristles outward, against the bottom of the folded sheet of the apple-pie bed, where one or the other of Captain Baster's feet was sure to find it. The Terror did not care which foot was successful.

Then inspiration failed them; the Terror took the cigarette-case from the dressing-table; they came quietly down the stairs and out of the inn.

As they turned up the street the Terror said with modest if somewhat vengeful triumph: "There! you see things *do* occur to us." Then with his usual scrupulous fairness he added: "But it was Wiggins who set us going."

"I'm an ally; and he called me Freckles," said Wiggins vengefully; and once more he spurned the earth.

On their way home, half-way up the lane, where the trees arched most thickly overhead, they came to a patch of deepish mud which was too sheltered to have dried after the heavy rain of the day before.

"Mind the mud, Wiggins," said Erebus, mindful of his carelessness in the matter.

Wiggins walked gingerly along the side of it and said: "It wouldn't be a nice place to fall down in, would it?"

The Terror went on a few paces, stopped short, laughed a hard, sinister little laugh, and said: "Wiggins, you're a treasure!"

"What is it? What is it now?" said Erebus quickly.

"A little job of my own. It wouldn't do for you and Wiggins to have a hand in it, he'll swear so," said the Terror.

"Who'll swear?" said Erebus.

"The Cruncher. And you're a girl and Wiggins is too young to hear such language," said the Terror.

"Rubbish!" said Erebus sharply. "Tell us what it is."

The Terror shook his head.

"It's a beastly shame! I ought to help—I always do," cried Erebus in a bitterly aggrieved tone.

The Terror shook his head.

"All right," said Erebus. "Who wants to help in a stupid thing like that? But all the same you'll go and make a silly mull of it without me—you always do."

"You jolly well wait and see," said the Terror with calm confidence.

Erebus was still muttering darkly about piggishness when they reached the house.

They went into the drawing-room in a body and found Captain Baster still talking to their mother, in the middle, indeed, of a long story illustrating his prowess in a game of polo, on two three-hundred-guinea and one three-hundred-and-fifty-guinea ponies. He laid great stress on the prices he had paid for them.

When it came to an end, the Terror gave him his cigarette-case.

Mrs. Dangerfield observed this example of the thoughtfulness of her offspring with an air of doubtful surprise.

Captain Baster took the cigarette-case and said with hearty jocularity: "Thank you, Error—thank you. But why didn't you bring it to me, Terebus? Then you'd have earned that kiss I'm going to give you."

Erebus gazed at him with murderous eyes, and said in a sinister tone: "Oh, I helped to get it."

CHAPTER II

GUARDIAN ANGELS

At seven o'clock Captain Baster took his leave to dine at his inn. Of his own accord he promised faithfully to return at nine sharp. He left the house a proud and happy man, for he knew that he had been shining before Mrs. Dangerfield with uncommon brilliance.

He was not by any means blind to her charm and beauty, for though she was four years older than he, she contrived never to look less than two years younger, and that without any aid from the cosmetic arts. But he chiefly saw in her an admirable ladder to those social heights to which his ardent soul aspired to climb. She had but to return to the polite world from which the loss of her husband and her straightened circumstances had removed her, to find herself a popular woman with a host of friends in the exalted circles Captain Baster burned to adorn. Yet it must not for a moment be supposed that he was proposing a mercenary marriage for her; he was sure that she loved him, for he felt rather than knew that with women he was irresistible.

It was not love, however, that knitted Mrs. Dangerfield's brow in a troubled frown as she dressed; nor was it love that caused her to select to wear that evening one of her oldest and dowdiest gowns, a gown with which she had never been truly pleased. The troubled air did not leave her face during dinner; and it seemed to affect the Twins, for they, too, were gloomy. They were pleased, indeed, with the beginning of the campaign, but still very doubtful of success in the end. Where their interests were concerned their mother was of a firmness indeed hard to move.

Moreover, she kept looking at them in an odd considering fashion that disturbed them, especially at the Terror. Erebus in a pretty light frock of her mother's days of prosperity, which had been cut down and fitted to her, was a sight to brighten any one's eyes; but the sleeves of the dark coat which the Terror wore on Sundays and on gala evenings, bared a length of wrist distressing to a mother's eye.

The fine high spirits of Captain Baster were somewhat dashed by his failure to find his keys and open his portmanteau, since he would be unable to ravish Mrs. Dangerfield's eye that evening by his distinguished appearance in the unstained evening dress of an English gentleman. After a long hunt for the mislaid keys, in which the harried staff of The Plough took part, he made up his mind that he must appear before her, with all apologies, in the tweed suit he was wearing. It was a bitter thought, for in a tweed suit he could not really feel a conquering hero after eight o'clock at night.

Then he put his foot into a dress-boot full of cold water. It was a good water-tight boot; and it had faithfully retained all of the water its lining had not soaked up. The gallant officer said a good deal about its retentive properties to the mute boot.

At dinner be learned from Mrs. Pittaway that the obliging Terror had himself fetched the cigarette-case from his bedroom. A flash of intuition connected the Terror with the watered boot; and he begged her, with loud acerbity, never again to let any one—any one!!—enter his bedroom. Mrs. Pittaway objected that slops could not be emptied, or beds made without human intervention. He begged her, not perhaps unreasonably, not to talk like a fool; and she liked him none the better for his directness.

Food always soothed him; and he rose from his dinner in better spirits. As he rose from it, the Terror, standing among the overarching trees which made the muddy patch in the lane so dark, was drawing a clothes-line tight. It ran through the hedge that hid him to the hedge on the other side of the lane. There it was fastened to a stout stake; and he was fastening it to the lowest rail of a post and rails. At its tightest it rose a foot above the roadway just at the beginning of the mud-patch. It was at its tightest.

Heartened by his dinner and two extra whiskies and sodas, Captain Baster set out for Colet House at a brisk pace. As he moved through the bracing autumn air, his spirits rose yet higher; that night—that very night he would crown Mrs. Dangerfield's devotion with his avowal of an answering passion. He pressed forward swiftly like a conqueror; and like a conqueror he whistled. Then he found the clothes-line, suddenly, pitched forward and fell, not heavily, for the mud was thick, but sprawling. He rose, oozy and dripping, took a long breath, and the welkin shuddered as it rang.

The Terror did not shudder; he was going home like the wind.

Having sent Erebus to bed at a few minutes to nine Mrs. Dangerfield waited restlessly for her tardy guest, her charming face still set in a troubled frown. Her woman's instinct assured her that Captain Baster would propose that night; and she dreaded it. Two or three times she rose and walked up and down the room; and when she saw her deep, dark, troubled eyes in the two old, almost giltless round mirrors, they did not please her as they usually did. Those eyes were one of the sources from which had sprung Captain Baster's attraction to her.

But there were the Twins; she longed to do so many useful, needful things for them; and marriage with Captain Baster was the way of doing them. She told herself that he would make an excellent stepfather and husband; that under his unfortunate manner were a good heart and sterling qualities. She assured herself that she had the power to draw them out; once he was her husband, she would change him. But still she was ill at ease. Perhaps, in her heart of hearts, she was doubtful of her power to make a silk purse out of rhinoceros hide.

When at last a note came from The Plough to say that he was unfortunately prevented from coming that evening, but would come next morning to take her for a walk, she was filled with so extravagant a relief that it frightened her. She sat down and wrote out a telegram to her brother, rang for old Sarah, their trusty hard-working maid, and bade her tell the Terror, who had slipped quietly upstairs to bed at one minute to nine, to send it off in the morning. She did not wish to take the chance of not waking and despatching it as early as possible. She must have advice; and Sir Maurice Falconer was not only a shrewd man of the world, but he would also advise her with the keenest regard for her interests. She tried not to hope that he would find marriage with Captain Baster incompatible with them.

Captain Baster awoke in less than his usual cheerfulness. He thought for a while of the Terror and boots and mud with a gloomy unamiability. Then he rose and betook himself to his toilet. In the middle of it he missed his shaving-brush. He hunted for it furiously; he could have sworn that he had taken it out of his portmanteau. He did swear, but not to any definite fact. There was nothing for it: he must expose his tender chin to the cruel razor of a village barber.

Then he disliked the look of his tweed suit; all traces of mud had not vanished from it. In one short night it had lost its pristine freshness. This and the ordeal before his chin made his breakfast gloomy; and soon after it he entered the barber's shop with the air of one who has abandoned hope Later he came out of it with his roving black eye full of tears of genuine feeling; his scraped chin was smarting cruelly and unattractive in patches—red patches. At the door the breath-less, excited and triumphant maid of the inn accosted him with the news that she had just found his keys and his shaving-brush under the mattress of his bed. He looked round the village of Little Deeping blankly; it suddenly seemed to him a squalid place.

None the less it was a comforting thought that he would not be put to the expense of having his portmanteau broken open and fitted with a new lock, for his great wealth had never weakened the essential thriftiness of his soul. Half an hour later, in changed tweeds but with unchanged chin, he took his way to Colet House, thinking with great unkindness of his future stepson. As he drew near it he saw that that stepson was awaiting him at the garden gate; nearer still he saw that he was awaiting him with an air of ineffable serenity.

The Terror politely opened the gate for him, and with a kind smile asked him if he had slept well.

The red blood of the Basters boiled in the captain's veins, and he said somewhat thickly: "Look here, my lad, I don't want any more of your tricks! You play another on me, and I'll give you the soundest licking you ever had in your life!"

The serenity on the Terror's face broke up into an expression of the deepest pain: "Whatever's the matter?" he said in a tone of amazement. "I thought you loved a joke. You said you did—yesterday—at tea."

"You try it on again!" said Captain Baster.

"Now, whatever has put your back up?" said the Terror in a tone of even greater amazement. "Was it the apple-pie bed, or the lost keys, or the water in the boot, or the clothes-line across the road?"

It was well that the Terror could spring with a cat's swiftness: Captain Baster's boot missed him by a hair's breadth.

The Terror ran round the house, in at the back door and up to the bedroom of Erebus.

"Waxy?" he cried joyously. "He's black in the face! I told him he said he loved a joke."

Erebus only growled deep down in her throat. She was bitterly aggrieved that she had not had a hand in Captain Baster's downfall the night before. The Terror had awakened her to tell her joyfully of his glorious exploit and of the shuddering welkin.

He paid no heed to the rumbling of her discontent; he said: "Now, you quite understand. You'll stick to them like a leech. You won't give him any chance of talking to Mum alone. It's most important."

"I understand. But what's that? Anybody could do it," she

Edgar Jepson

said in a tone of extreme bitterness. "It's you that's getting all the real fun."

"But you'll be able to make yourself beastly disagreeable, if you're careful," said the Terror.

"Of course, I shall. But what's that? I tell you what it is: I'm going to have my proper share of the real fun. The first chance I get, I'm going to stone him—so there!" said Erebus fiercely.

"All right. But it doesn't seem quite the thing for a girl to do," said the Terror in a judicial tone.

"Rats!" said Erebus.

It was well that Mrs. Dangerfield kept Captain Baster waiting; it gave the purple tinge, which was heightening his floridness somewhat painfully, time to fade. When she did come to him, he was further annoyed by the fact that Erebus came too, and with a truculent air announced her intention of accompanying them. Mrs. Dangerfield was surprised; Erebus seldom showed any taste for such a gentle occupation. Also she was relieved; she did not want Captain Baster to propose before she had taken counsel with her brother.

Captain Baster started in a gloomy frame of mind; he did not try to hide from himself the fact that Mrs. Dangerfield had lost some of her charm: she was the mother of the Terror. He found, too, that his instinctive distaste for the company of Erebus was not ungrounded. She was a nuisance; she would talk about wet boots; the subject seemed to fascinate her. Then, when at last he recovered his spirits, grew once more humorous, and even rose to the proposing point, there was no getting rid of her. She was impervious to hints; she refused, somewhat pertly, to pause and gather the luscious blackberries. How could a man be his humorous self in these circumstances? He felt that his humor was growing strained, losing its delightful lightness.

Then the accident: it was entirely Erebus' own fault (he could swear it) that he tripped over her foot and pitched among those infernal brambles. Her howls of anguish were all humbug: he had not hurt her ankle (he could swear it); there was not a tear. The moment he offered, furiously, to carry her, she walked without a vestige of a limp.

Mrs. Dangerfield had no right to look vexed with him; if one brought up one's children like that—well. Certainly she was losing her charm; she was the mother of Erebus also.

His doubt, whether the mother of such children was the right kind of wife for him, had grown very serious indeed, when, as they drew near Colet House, a slim, tall young man of an extreme elegance and distinction came through the garden gate to meet them.

With a cry of "Uncle Maurice!" the crippled Erebus dashed to meet him with the light bounds of an antelope. Captain Baster could hardly believe his eyes; he knew the young man by sight, by name and by repute. It was Sir Maurice Falconer, a man he longed to boast his friend. With his aid a man might climb to the highest social peaks.

When Mrs. Dangerfield introduced him as her brother (he had never dreamed it) he could not believe his good fortune. But why had he not learned this splendid fact before? Why had he been kept in the dark? He did not reflect that he had been so continuously busy making confidences about himself, his possessions and his exploits to her that he had given her the smallest opportunities of telling him anything about herself.

Edgar Jepson

But he was not one to lose a golden opportunity; he set about making up for lost time with a will; and never had he so thoroughly demonstrated his right to the name of Pallybaster. His friendliness was overwhelming. Before the end of lunch he had invited Sir Maurice to dine with him at his mess, to dine with him at two of his clubs, to shoot with him, to ride a horse of his in the forthcoming regimental steeplechases, to go with him on a yachting cruise in the Mediterranean.

All through the afternoon his friendliness grew and grew. He could not bear that any one else should have a word with Sir Maurice. The Twins were intolerable with their interruptions, their claims on their uncle's attention. They disgusted Captain Baster: when he became their stepfather, it would be his first task to see that they learned a respectful silence in the presence of their elders.

He never gave a thought to his proposal; he sought no occasion to make it. Captain Baster's love was of his life a thing apart, but his social aspirations were the chief fact of his existence. Besides, there was no haste; he knew that Mrs. Dangerfield was awaiting his avowal with a passionate eagerness; any time would do for that. But he must seize the fleeting hour and bind Sir Maurice to himself by the bond of the warmest friendship.

Again and again he wondered how Sir Maurice could give his attention to the interrupting exacting Twins, when he had a man of the world, humorous, knowing, wealthy, to talk to. He tried to make opportunities for him to escape from them; Sir Maurice missed those opportunities; he did not seem to see them. In truth Captain Baster was a little disappointed in Sir Maurice: he did not find him frankly responsive: polite— yes; indeed, politeness could go no further. But he lacked warmth. After all he had not pinned him down to the definite acceptance of a single invitation.

When, at seven o'clock, he tore himself away with the hearty assurance that he would be back at nine sharp, he was not sure that he had made a bosom friend. He felt that the friendship might need clenching.

As the front door shut behind him, Sir Maurice wiped his brow with the air of one who has paused from exhausting toil: "I feel sticky—positively sticky," he said. "Oh, Erebus, you do have gummy friends! I thought we should never get rid of him. I thought he'd stuck himself to us for the rest of our natural lives."

Mrs. Dangerfield smiled; and the Terror said in a tone of deep meaning: "That's what he's up to."

"He's not a friend of mine!" cried Erebus hotly.

"We call him the Cruncher—because of his teeth," said the Terror.

"Then beware, Erebus—beware! You are young and possibly savory," said Sir Maurice.

"You children had better go and get ready for dinner," said Mrs. Dangerfield.

The Twins went to the door. On the threshold Erebus turned and said: "It's Mum he wants to crunch up—not me."

The bolt shot, she fled through the door.

Sir Maurice looked at his sister and said softly:

"Oho! I see—heroism. That was what you wanted to consult me about." Then he laid his hand on her shoulder affectionately and added: "It won't do, Anne—it won't do at all. I am convinced of it."

"Do you think so?" said Mrs. Dangerfield in a tone in which disappointment and relief were very nicely blended.

"Think? I'm sure of it," said Sir Maurice in a tone of complete conviction.

"But the children; he could do so much for the children,' pleaded Mrs. Dangerfield.

"He could, but he wouldn't. That kind of bounder never does any one any good but himself. No, no; the children are right in calling him the Cruncher. He would just crunch you up; and it is a thousand times better for them to have an uncrunched mother than all the money that ever came out of pickles."

"Well, you know best. You do understand these things," said Mrs. Dangerfield; and she sighed.

"I do understand Basters," said Sir Maurice in a confident tone.

Mrs. Dangerfield ran up-stairs to dress, on the light feet of a girl; a weight oppressive, indeed, had been lifted from her spirit.

Dinner was a very bright and lively meal, though now and again a grave thoughtfulness clouded the spirits of Erebus. Once Sir Maurice asked her the cause of it. She only shook her head.

Captain Baster ate his dinner in a sizzling excitement: he knew that he had made a splendid first impression; he was burning to deepen it. But on his eager way back to Colet

House, he walked warily, feeling before him with his stick for clotheslines. He came out of the dark lane into the broad turf road, which runs across the common to the house, with a strong sense of relief and became once more his hearty care-free self.

There was not enough light to display the jaunty air with which he walked in all its perfection; but there seemed to be light enough for more serious matters, for a stone struck him on the thigh with considerable force. He had barely finished the jump of pained surprise with which he greeted it, when another stone whizzed viciously past his head; then a third struck him on the shoulder.

With the appalling roar of a bull of Bashan the gallant officer dashed in the direction whence, he judged, the stones came. He was just in time to stop a singularly hard stone with his marble brow. Then he found a gorse-bush (by tripping over a root) a gorse-bush which seemed unwilling to release him from its stimulating, not to say prickly, embrace. As he wallowed in it another stone found him, his ankle-bone.

He wrenched himself from the embrace of the gorse-bush, found his feet and realized that there was only one thing to do. He tore along the turf road to Colet House as hard as he could pelt. A stone struck the garden gate as he opened it. He did not pause to ring; he opened the front door, plunged heavily across the hall into the drawing-room. The Terror formed the center of a domestic scene; he was playing draughts with his Uncle Maurice.

Captain Baster glared at him with unbelieving eyes and gasped: "I—I made sure it was that young whelp!"

This sudden violent entry of a bold but disheveled hussar produced a natural confusion; Mrs. Dangerfield, Sir Maurice

Edgar Jepson

and the Terror sprang to their feet, asking with one voice what had befallen him.

Captain Baster sank heavily on to a chair and instantly sprang up from it with a howl as he chanced on several tokens of the gorse-bush's clinging affection.

"I've been stoned—stoned by some hulking scoundrels on the common!" he cried; and he displayed the considerable bump rising on his marble brow.

Mrs. Dangerfield was full of concern and sympathy; Sir Maurice was cool, interested but cool; he did not blaze up into the passionate indignation of a bosom friend.

"How many of them were there?" said the Terror.

"From the number of stones they threw I should think there were a dozen," said Captain Baster; and he panted still.

The Terror looked puzzled.

"I know—I know what it is!" cried Mrs. Dangerfield with an illuminating flash of womanly intuition. "You've been humorous with some of the villagers!"

"No, no! I haven't joked with a single one of them!" cried Captain Baster. "But I'll teach the scoundrels a lesson! I'll put the police on them tomorrow morning. I'll send for a detective from London. I'll prosecute them."

Then Erebus entered, her piquant face all aglow: "I couldn't find your handkerchief anywhere, Mum. It took me ever such a time," she said, giving it to her.

The puzzled air faded from the Terror's face; and he said in a tone of deep meaning: "Have you been running to find it? You're quite out of breath."

For a moment a horrid suspicion filled the mind of Captain Baster. . . . But no: it was impossible—a child in whose veins flowed some of the bluest blood in England. Besides, her slender arms could never have thrown the stones as straight and hard as that.

On the other hand Sir Maurice appeared to have lost for once his superb self-possession; he was staring at his beautiful niece with his mouth slightly open. He muttered; something about finding his handkerchief, and stumbled out of the room. They heard a door bang up-stairs; then, through the ceiling, they heard a curious drumming sound. It occurred to the Terror that it might be the heels of Sir Maurice on the floor.

Mrs. Dangerfield rang for old Sarah and instructed her to pull the gorse prickles out of Captain Baster's clothes. She had nearly finished when Sir Maurice returned. He carried a handkerchief in his hand, and he had recovered his superb self-possession; but he seemed somewhat exhausted.

Captain Baster was somewhat excessive in the part of the wounded hero; and for a while he continued to talk ferociously of the vengeance he would wreak on the scoundrelly villagers. But after a while he forgot his pricks and bruises to bask in the presence of Sir Maurice; and he plied him with unflagging friendliness for the rest of the evening.

The Twins were allowed to sit up till ten o'clock since their Uncle Maurice was staying with them; and since the Terror was full of admiration and approval of Erebus' strenuous endeavor to instil into Captain Baster the perils and drawbacks of stepfatherhood, he brushed out her abundant hair

Edgar Jepson

for her, an office he sometimes performed when she was in high favor with him. As he did it she related gleefully the stoning of their enemy.

When she had done, he said warmly: "It was ripping. But the nuisance is: he doesn't know it was you who did it, and so it's rather wasted."

"Don't you worry: I'll let him know sometime to-morrow," said Erebus firmly.

"Yes; but he's awfully waxy: suppose he prosecutes you?" said the Terror doubtfully.

Erebus considered the point; then she said: "I don't think he'd do that; he'd look so silly being stoned by a girl. Anyhow, I'll chance it."

"All right," said the Terror. "It's worth chancing it to put him off marrying mother. And of course Uncle Maurice is here. He'll see nothing serious happens."

"Of course he will," said Erebus.

It must have been that the unflagging friendliness of Captain Baster had weighed on their uncle's mind, for Erebus, coming softly on him from behind as he leaned over the garden gate after breakfast, heard him singing to himself, and paused to listen to his song.

It went:

> *"Where did his colonel dig him up,*
> *So young, so fair, so sweet,*
> *With his shining nose, and his square, square toes?*
> *Was it Wapping or Basinghall Street?"*

He was so pleased with the effort that he sang it over to himself, softly, twice with an air of deep satisfaction; and twice the moving but silent lips of Erebus repeated it.

He was silent; and she said: "Oh, uncle! It's splendid!"

Sir Maurice started and turned sharply: "You tell any one, little pitcher, and I'll pull your long ears," he said amiably.

Erebus made no rash promises; she gazed at him with inscrutable eyes; then nodding toward a figure striding swiftly over the common, she said: "Here he comes."

Sir Maurice gained the threshold of the front door in two bounds, paused and cried: "I'm going back to bed! Tell him I'm in bed!"

He vanished, slamming the door behind him.

Captain Baster asked for Sir Maurice cheerfully; and his face fell when Erebus told him that he had gone back to bed. Mrs. Dangerfield, informed of her brother's shrinking, had to be very firm with his new friend to induce him to go for a walk with her and Erebus. He showed an inclination to linger about the house till his sun should rise.

Then he tried to shorten the walk; but in this matter too Mrs. Dangerfield was firm. She did not bring him back till half past twelve, only to learn that Sir Maurice was very busy writing letters in his bedroom. Captain Baster hoped for an invitation to lunch (he hinted as much) but he was disappointed. In the end he returned to The Plough, chafing furiously; he felt that his morning had been barren.

He was soon back at Colet House, but too late; Sir Maurice had started on a walk with the Terror. Captain Baster said cheerily that he would overtake them, and set out briskly to do so. He walked hard enough to compass that end; and it is probable that he would have had a much better chance of succeeding, had not Erebus sent him eastward whereas Sir Maurice and the Terror had gone westward.

Captain Baster returned to Colet House in time for tea; and his heart swelled big within him to learn that Mrs. Dangerfield had invited some friends to meet him and her brother. Here was his chance to shine, to show Sir Maurice his social mettle.

He could have wished that the party had been larger. They were only a dozen all told: Mr. Carruthers, the squire of Little Deeping, the vicar and his wife, the higher mathematician, father of Wiggins, Mrs. Blenkinsop and Mrs. Morton, and Wiggins himself, who had spent most of the afternoon with Erebus. Captain Baster would have preferred thirty or forty, but none the less he fell to work with a will.

Mrs. Dangerfield had taken advantage of the Indian summer afternoon to have tea in the garden; and it gave him room to expand. He was soon the life and soul of the gathering. He was humorous with the vicar about the church, and with the squire about the dulling effect of the country on the intelligence. He tried to be humorous with Mr. Carrington, the higher mathematician, whom he took to have retired from some profession or business. This was so signal a failure that he dropped humor and became important, telling them of his flat in town and his country-house, their size and their expensive furniture; he told them about his motor-cars, his exploits at regimental cricket, at polo and at golf.

He patronized every one with a splendid affability, every one except Sir Maurice; and him he addressed, with a flattering air of perfect equality, as "Maurice, old boy," or "Maurice, old chap," or plain "Maurice." He did shine; his agreeable exertions threw him into a warm perspiration; his nose shone especially; and they all hated him.

The Twins were busy handing round tea-cups and cakes, but they were aware that their mother's tea-party was a failure. As a rule her little parties were so pleasant with their atmosphere of friendliness; and her guests went away pleased with themselves, her and one another. The Terror was keenly alive to the effect of Captain Baster; and a faint persistent frown troubled his serenity. Erebus was more dimly aware that her enemy was spoiling the party. Only Sir Maurice and Mr. Carrington really enjoyed the humorist; and Sir Maurice's enjoyment was mingled with vexation.

Every one had finished their tea; and they were listening to Captain Baster in a dull aggravation and blank silence, when he came to the end of his panegyric on his possessions and accomplishments, and remembered his grievance. Forthwith he related at length the affair of the night before: how he had been stoned by a dozen hulking scoundrels on the common. When he came to the end of it, he looked round for sympathy.

His audience wore a strained rather than sympathetic air, all of them except the higher mathematician who had turned away and was coughing violently.

The vicar broke the silence; he said: "Er—er—yes; most extraordinary. But I don't think it could have been the villagers. They're—er—very peaceful people."

"It must have been some rowdies from Rowington," said the squire in the loud tone of a man trying to persuade his hearers that he believed what he said.

Erebus rose and walked to the gravel path; their eyes fixed in an incredulous unwinking stare.

She picked up three pebbles from the path, choosing them with some care. The first pebble hit the weathercock, which rose above the right gable of the house, plumb in the middle; the second missed its tail by a couple of inches; the third hit its tail, and the weathercock spun round as if a vigorous gale were devoting itself to its tail only.

"That's where I meant to hit it the first time," said Erebus with a little explanatory wave of her hand; and she returned to her seat.

The silence that fell was oppressive. Captain Baster gazed earnestly at Erebus, his roving black eyes fixed in an incredulous unwinking stare.

"That shows you the danger of jumping to hasty conclusions," said the higher mathematician in his clear agreeable voice. "I made sure it was the Terror."

"So did I," said the vicar.

"I'd have bet on it," said the squire.

The silence fell again. Mechanically Captain Baster rubbed the blue bump on his marble brow.

Erebus broke the silence; she said: "Has any one heard Wiggins' new song?"

The squire, hastily and thoughtlessly, cried: "No! Let's hear it!"

"Come on, Wiggins!" cried the vicar heartily.

They felt that the situation was saved.

Sir Maurice did not share their relief; he knew what was coming, knew it in the depths of his horror-stricken heart. He ground his teeth softly and glared at the piquant and glowing face of his niece as if he could have borne the earth's suddenly opening and swallowing her up.

The blushing Wiggins held back a little, and kicked his left foot with his right. Then pushed forward by the eager Terror, to whom Erebus had chanted the song before lunch, he stepped forward and in his dear shrill treble, sang, slightly out of tune:

> *"Where did his colonel dig him up,*
> *So young, so fair, so sweet,*
> *With his shining nose, and his square, square toes?*
> *Was it Wapping or Basinghall Street?"*

As he sang Wiggins looked artlessly at Captain Baster; as he finished everybody was looking at Captain Baster's boots; his feet required them square-toed.

Captain Baster's face was a rich rose-pink; he, glared round the frozen circle now trying hard not to look at his boots; he saw the faces melt into irrepressible smiles; he looked to Sir Maurice, the

[Transcriber's note: page 53 missing from book.]

CHAPTER III

AND THE CATS' HOME

[Transcriber's note: page 54 missing from book]

Wiggins," said Sir Maurice amiably. "And if we start apologizing, there will be no end to it. I should have to come in myself as the maker of the bomb who carelessly left it lying about."

"It was certainly a happy effort," said the vicar, smiling. Then he changed the subject firmly, saying: "We're going to London next week; perhaps you could recommend a play to us to go to, Sir Maurice."

A faint ripple of grateful relaxation ran round the circle and presently it was clear that in taking himself off Captain Baster had lifted a wet blanket of quite uncommon thickness from the party. They were talking easily and freely; and Mrs. Dangerfield and Sir Maurice were seeing to it that every one, even Mrs. Blenkinsop and Mrs. Morton, were getting their little chances of shining. The Twins and Wiggins slipped away; and their elders talked the more at their ease for their going. In the end the little gathering which Captain Baster had so nearly crushed, broke up in the best of spirits, all the guests in a state of amiable satisfaction with Mrs.

Dangerfield, themselves and one another.

After they had gone Sir Maurice and Mrs. Dangerfield discussed the exploits of Erebus; and he did his best to abate her distress at the two onslaughts his violent niece had made on a guest. The Terror was also doing his best in the matter: with unbending firmness he prevented Erebus, eager to enjoy her uncle's society, from returning to the house till it was time to dress for dinner. He wished to give his mother time to get over the worst of her annoyance.

Thanks to their efforts Mrs. Dangerfield did not rebuke her violent daughter with any great severity. But even so, Erebus did not receive these milder rebukes in the proper meek spirit. Unlike the philosophic Terror, who for the most part accepted his mother's just rebukes, after a doubtful exploit, with a disarming sorrowful air, Erebus must always make out a case for herself; and she did so now.

Displaying an injured air, she took the ground that Captain Baster was not really a guest on the previous evening, since he was making a descent on the house uninvited, and therefore he did not come within the sphere of the laws of hospitality.

"Besides he never behaved like a guest," she went on in a bitterly aggrieved tone. "He was always making himself objectionable to every one—especially to me. And if he was always trying to score off me, I'd a perfect right to score off him. And anyhow, I wasn't going to let him marry you without doing everything I could to stop it. He'd be a perfectly beastly stepfather—you know he would."

This was an aspect of the matter Mrs. Dangerfield had no desire to discuss; and flushing a little, she contented herself with closing the discussion by telling Erebus not to do it again. She knew that however bitterly Erebus might protest against a just rebuke, she would take it sufficiently to heart. She was sure that she would not stone another guest.

With the departure of Captain Baster peace settled on Colet House; and Sir Maurice enjoyed very much his three days' stay. The Twins, though they were in that condition of subdued vivacity into which they always fell after a signal exploit that came to their mother's notice, were very pleasant companions; and the peaceful life and early hours of Little Deeping were grateful after the London whirl. Also he had many talks with his sister on the matter of settling down in life, a course of action she frequently urged on him.

When he went the Twins felt a certain dulness. It was not acute boredom; they were preserved from that by the fact that the Terror went every morning to study the classics with the vicar, and Erebus learned English and French with her mother. Their afternoon leisure, therefore, rarely palled on them.

One afternoon, as they came out of the house after lunch, Erebus suggested that they should begin by ambushing Wiggins. They went, therefore, toward Mr. Carrington's house which stood nearly a mile away on the outskirts of Little Deeping, and watched it from the edge of the common. They saw their prey in the garden; and he tried their patience by staying there for nearly a quarter of an hour.

Then he came briskly up the road to the common. Their eyes began to shine with the expectation of immediate triumph, when, thirty yards from the common's edge, in a sudden access of caution, he bolted for covert and disappeared in the gorse sixty yards away on their left. They fell noiselessly back, going as quickly as concealment permitted, to cut him off. They were successful. They caught him crossing an open space, yelled "Bang!" together; and in accordance with the rules of the game Wiggins fell to the ground.

They scalped him with yells of such a piercing triumph that the immemorial oaks for a quarter of a mile round emptied themselves hastily of the wood-pigeons feeding on their acorns.

Wiggins rose gloomily, gloomily took from his knicker-bockers pocket his tattered and grimy notebook, gloomily made an entry in it, and gloomily said: "That makes you two games ahead." Then he spurned the earth and added: "I'm going to have a bicycle."

The Twins looked at each other darkly; Erebus scowled, and a faint frown broke the ineffable serenity of the Terror's face.

"There'll be no living with Wiggins now, he'll be so cocky," said Erebus bitterly.

"Oh, no; he won't," said the Terror. "But we ought to have bicycles, too. We want them badly. We never get really far from the village. We always get stopped on the way—rats, or something." And his guileless, dreamy blue eyes swept the distant autumn hills with a look of yearning.

"There are orchards over there where they don't know us," said Erebus wistfully.

"We *must* have bicycles. I've been thinking so for a long time," said the Terror.

"We must have the moon!" said Erebus with cold scorn.

"Bicycles aren't so far away," said the Terror sagely.

They moved swiftly across the common. Erebus poured forth a long monotonous complaint about the lack of bicycles, which, for them, made this Cosmic All a mere time-honored cheat. With ears impervious to his sister's vain lament, the Terror strode on serenely thoughtful, pondering this pressing problem. Now and again, for obscure but profound reasons, Wiggins spurned the earth and proceeded by leaps and bounds.

Possibly it was the monotonous plaint of his sister which caused the Terror to say: "I've got a penny. We'll go and get some bull's-eyes."

At any rate the monotonous plaint ceased.

They had returned on their steps across the common, and were nearing the village, when they met three small boys. One of them carried a kitten.

Erebus stopped short. "What are you going to do with that kitten, Billy Beck?" she said.

"We be goin' to drown 'im in the pond," said Billy Beck in the important tones of an executioner.

Erebus sprang; and the kitten was in her hands. "You're not going to do anything of the sort, you little beast!" she said.

The round red face of Billy Beck flushed redder with rage and disappointment, and he howled:

"Gimme my kitty! Mother says she won't 'ave 'im about the 'ouse, an' I could drown 'im."

"You won't have him," said Erebus.

Billy Beck and his little brothers, robbed of their simple joy, burst into blubbering roar of "It's ourn! It ain't yourn! It's ourn!"

"It isn't! A kitten isn't any one's to drown!" cried Erebus.

The Terror gazed at Erebus and Billy Beck with judicial eyes, the cold personification of human justice. Erebus edged away from him ready to fly, should human justice intervene actively. The Terror put his hand in his pocket and fumbled. He drew out a penny, and looked at it earnestly. He was weighing the respective merits of justice and bull's-eyes.

"Here's a penny for your kitten. You can buy bull's-eyes with it," he said with a sigh, and held out the coin.

A sudden greed sparkled in Billy Beck's tearful eyes. "'E's worth more'n a penny—a kitty like 'im!" he blubbered.

"Not to drown. It's all you'll get," said the Terror curtly. He tossed the penny to Billy's feet, turned on his heel and went back across the common away from the village. Some of the brightness faded out of the faces of Erebus and Wiggins.

"I wouldn't have given him a penny. He was only going to drown the kitten," said Erebus in a grudging tone.

"It was his kitten. We couldn't take it without paying for it," said the Terror coldly.

Erebus followed him, cuddling the kitten and talking to it as she went.

Presently Wiggins spurned the earth and said, "There ought to be a home for kittens nobody wants—and puppies."

Edgar Jepson

The Terror stopped short, and said: "By Jove! There's Aunt Amelia!"

Erebus burst into a bitter complaint of the stinginess of Aunt Amelia, who had more money than all the rest of the family put together, and yet never rained postal orders on deserving nieces and nephews, but spent it all on horrid cats' homes.

"That's just it," said the Terror in a tone of considerable animation. "Come along; I want you to write a letter."

"I'm not going to write any disgusting letter!" cried Erebus hotly.

"Then you're not going to get any bicycle. Come on. I'll look out the words in the dictionary, and Wiggins can help because, seeing so much of his father, he's got into the way of using grammar. It'll be useful. Come on!"

They came on, Wiggins, as always, deeply impressed by the importance of being a helper of the Twins, for they were in their fourteenth year, and only ten brief wet summers had passed over his own tousled head, Erebus clamoring to have her suddenly aroused curiosity gratified. Practise had made the Terror's ears impervious at will to his sister's questions, which were frequent and innumerable. Without a word of explanation he led the way home; without a word he set her down at the dining-room table with paper and ink before her, and sat down himself on the opposite side of it, a dictionary in his hand and Wiggins by his side.

Then he said coldly: "Now don't make any blots, or you'll have to do it all over again."

"I never make blots! It's you that makes blots!" cried Erebus, ruffled. "Mr. Etheridge says I write ever so much better than you do. Ever so much better."

"That's why you're writing the letter and not me," said the Terror coldly. "Fire away: 'My dear Aunt Amelia'—I say, Wiggins, what's the proper words for 'awfully keen'?"

"'Keen' is 'interested'—I don't know how many 'r's' there are in 'interested'—and 'awfully' is an awfully difficult word," said Wiggins, pondering.

The Terror looked up "interested" in the dictionary with a laborious painfulness, and announced triumphantly that there was but a single "r" in it; then he said, "What's the right word for 'awfully,' Wiggins? Buck up!"

"'Tremendously,'" said Wiggins with the air of a successful Columbus.

"That's it," said the Terror. "'My dear Aunt Amelia: I have often heard that you are tremendously interested in cats' homes'"—

"I should think you had!" said Erebus.

"Now don't jabber, please; just stick to the writing," said the Terror. "I've got to make this letter a corker; and how can I think if you jabber?"

Erebus made a hideous grimace and bent to her task.

"'Little Deeping wants a cats' home awfully'—no: 'tremendously.' I like that word 'tremendously'; it means something," said the Terror.

"You're jabbering yourself now," said Erebus unpleasantly.

Ruffling his fair hair in the agony of composition, the Terror continued: "'The quantity of kittens that are drowned is horrible'—that ought to fetch her; kittens are so much nicer than cats—'and I have been thinking'—Oughtn't you to put in some stops?"

"I'm putting in stops—lots," said Erebus contemptuously.

"'I have been thinking—that if you wanted to have a cats' home here'—What's the right word for 'running a thing,' Wiggins?"

Wiggins frowned deeply; a number of his freckles seemed to run into one another.

"There is a word 'overseer'—slaves have them," he said cautiously.

The Terror sought that word painfully in the dictionary, spelled it out, and continued: "'I could overseer it for you. I have got my eye on a building which would suit us tremendously well. But these things cost money, and it would not be any use starting with less than thirty pounds'—

"Thirty pounds! My goodness!" cried Erebus; and her eyes opened wide.

"We may as well go the whole hog," said the Terror philosophically. "Go on: 'Or else just as the cats get to be happy and feel it was a real home—' What's the word for 'bust up,' Wiggins?"

"Burst up," said Wiggins without hesitation.

"No, no; not the grammar—the right word! Oh, I know; 'go bankrupt'—'it might go bankrupt. So it you would like to have a cats' home here and send me some money, I will start it at once. Your affectionate nephew, Hyacinth Wolfram Dangerfield.' There!" said the Terror with a sigh of relief.

"But you've left me out altogether," said Erebus in a suddenly aggrieved tone.

"I should jolly well think I had! You know that ever since you stayed with Aunt Amelia, and taught her parrot to say 'Dam,' she won't have anything to do with you," said the Terror firmly.

"There's no pleasing some people," said Erebus mournfully. "When I went there the silly old parrot couldn't say a thing; and when I came away, he could say 'Dam! Dam! Dam!' from morning till night without making a mistake."

"It's a word people don't like," said the Terror.

"Well, I and the parrot meant a dam in a river. I told Aunt Amelia so," said Erebus firmly.

"She might not believe you; she doesn't know how truthfully we've been brought up," said the Terror. "Go on; sign my name to the letter."

"That's forgery. You ought to sign your name yourself," said Erebus.

"No; you write my name better than I do; and it will go better with the rest of the letter. Sign away," said the Terror firmly.

Erebus signed away, and then she said: "But what good's the money going to be to us, if we've got to spend it on a silly old cats' home? It only means a lot of trouble."

The guilelessness deepened and deepened on the Terror's face. "Well, you see, there aren't many cats in Little Deeping—not enough to fill a cats' home decently," he said slowly. "We should have to have bicycles to collect them—from Great Deeping, and Muttle Deeping, and farther off."

Erebus gasped; and the light of understanding illumined her charming face, as she cried in a tone of awe not untinctured with admiration: "Well, you do think of things!"

"I have to," said the Terror. "If I didn't we should never have a single thing."

The Terror procured a stamp from Mrs. Dangerfield. He did not tell her of the splendid scheme he was promoting; he only said that he had thought he would write to Aunt Amelia. Mrs. Dangerfield was pleased with him for his thought: she wished him to stand well with his great-aunt, since she was a rich woman without children of her own. She did not, indeed, suggest that the letter should be shown to her, though she suspected that it contained some artless request. She thought it better that the Terror should write to his great-aunt to make requests rather than not write at all.

The letter posted, the Twins resumed the somewhat jerky tenor of their lives. Erebus was full of speculations about the changes in their lives those bicycles would bring about; she would pause in the very middle of some important enterprise to discuss the rides they would take on them, the orchards that those machines would bring within their reach. But the Terror would have none of it; his calm philosophic mind forbade him to discuss his chickens before they were hatched.

Since her philanthropy was confined entirely to cats, it is not remarkable that philanthropy, and not intelligence, was the chief characteristic of Lady Ryehampton. As the purport of her great-nephew's letter slowly penetrated her mind, a broad and beaming smile of gratification spread slowly over her large round face; and as she handed the letter to Miss Hendersyde, her companion, she cried in unctuous tones: "The dear boy! So young, but already enthusiastic about great things!"

Miss Hendersyde looked at her employer patiently; she foresaw that she was going to have to struggle with her to save her from being once more victimized. She had come to suspect anything that stirred Lady Ryehampton to a noble phrase. Her eyes brightened with humorous appreciation as she read the letter of Erebus; and when she came to the end of it she opened her mouth to point out that Little Deeping was one of the last places in England to need a cats' home. Then she bethought herself of the whole situation, shut her mouth with a little click, and her face went blank.

Then she breathed a short silent prayer for forgiveness, smiled and said warmly: "It's really wonderful. You must have inspired him with that enthusiasm yourself."

"I suppose I must," said Lady Ryehampton with an air of satisfaction. "And I must be careful not to discourage him."

Miss Hendersyde thought of the Terror's face, his charming sympathetic manners, and his darned knickerbockers. It was only right that some of Lady Ryehampton's money should go to him; indeed that money ought to be educating him at a good school. It was monstrous that the great bulk of it should be spent on cats; cats were all very well but human beings came first. And the Terror was such an attractive human being.

"Yes, it is a dreadful thing to discourage enthusiasm," she

said gravely.

Lady Ryehampton proceeded to discuss the question whether a cats' home could be properly started with thirty pounds, whether she had not better send fifty. Miss Hendersyde made her conscience quite comfortable by compromising: she said that she thought thirty was enough to begin with; that if more were needful, Lady Ryehampton could give it later. Lady Ryehampton accepted the suggestion.

Having set her employer's hand to the plow, Miss Hendersyde saw to it that she did not draw it back. Lady Ryehampton would spend money on cats, but she could not be hurried in the spending of it. But Miss Hendersyde kept referring to the Terror's enterprise all that day and the next morning, with the result that on the next afternoon Lady Ryehampton signed the check for thirty pounds. At Miss Hendersyde's suggestion she drew the money in cash; and Miss Hendersyde turned it into postal orders, for there is no bank at Little Deeping.

On the third morning the registered letter reached Colet House. The excited Erebus, who had been watching for the postman, received it from him, signed the receipt with trembling fingers, and dashed off with the precious packet to the Terror in the orchard.

The Terror took it from her with flawless serenity and opened it slowly.

But as he counted the postal orders, a faint flush covered his face; and he said in a somewhat breathless tone: "Thirty pounds—well!"

Erebus executed a short but Bacchic dance which she invented on the spur of that marvelous moment.

"It's splendid—splendid!" she cried. "It's the best thing you ever thought of!"

The Terror put the postal orders back into the envelope, and put the envelope into the breast pocket of his coat. A frown of the most thoughtful consideration furrowed his brow. Then he said firmly: "The first thing, to do is to get the bicycles. If once we've got them, no one will take them away from us."

"Of course they won't," said Erebus, with eager acceptance of his idea.

The breakfast-bell rang; and they went into the house, Erebus spurning the earth as she went, in the very manner of Wiggins.

In the middle of breakfast the Terror said in a casual tone and with a casual air, as if he was not greatly eager for the boon: "May we have the cow-house for our very own, Mum?"

"Oh, Terror! Surely you don't want to keep ferrets!" cried Mrs. Dangerfield, who lived in fear of the Terror's developing that inevitable boyish taste.

"Oh, no; but if we had the cow-house to do what we liked with, I think we could make a little pocket-money out of it."

"I am afraid you're growing terribly mercenary," said his mother; then she added with a sigh: "But I don't wonder at it, seeing how hard up you always are. You can have the cow-house. It's right at the end of the paddock—well away from the house—so that I don't see that you can do any harm with it whatever you do. But how are you going to make pocket-money out of it?"

"Oh, I haven't got it all worked out yet," said the Terror quickly. "But we'll tell you all about it when we have. Thanks ever so much for the cow-house."

For the rest of breakfast he left the conversation to Erebus.

The Terror was blessed with a masterly prudence uncommon indeed in a boy of his years. He changed but one of the six postal orders at Little Deeping—that would make talk enough—and then, having begged a holiday from the vicar, he took the train to Rowington, their market town, ten miles away, taking Erebus with him. There he changed three more postal orders; and then the Twins took their way to the bicycle shop, with hearts that beat high.

The Terror set about the purchase in a very careful leisurely way which, in any one else, would have exasperated the highly strung Erebus to the very limits of endurance; but where the Terror was concerned she had long ago learned the futility of exasperation. He began by an exhaustive examination of every make of bicycle in the shop; and he made it with a thoroughness that worried the eager bicycle-seller, one of those smart young men who pamper a chin's passion for receding by letting a straggly beard try to cover it, till his nerves were all on edge. Then the Terror, drawing a handful of sovereigns out of his pocket and gazing at them lovingly, seemed unable to make up his mind whether to buy two bicycles or one; and the bearded but chinless young man perspired with his eloquent efforts to demonstrate the advantage of buying two. He was quite weary when the persuaded Terror proceeded to develop the point that there must be a considerable reduction in price to the buyer of two bicycles. Then he made his offer: he would give fourteen pounds for two eight-pound-ten bicycles. His serenity was quite unruffled by the seller's furious protests. Then the real struggle began. The Terror came out of it with two bicycles, two lamps, two bells and two baskets of a size to hold a cat; the seller came out of it with fifteen pounds; and the triumphant Twins wheeled their machines out of the shop.

The Terror stood still and looked thoughtfully up and down High Street. Then he said: "We've saved the cats' home quite two pounds."

"Yes," said Erebus.

"And it's made me awfully hungry and thirsty doing it," said the Terror.

"It must have—arguing like that," said Erebus quickly; and her eyes brightened as she caught his drift.

"Well, I think the home ought to pay for refreshment. It's a long ride home," said the Terror.

"Of course it ought," said Erebus with decision.

Without more ado they wheeled their bicycles down the street to a confectioner's shop, propped them up carefully against the curb, and entered the shop with an important moneyed air.

At the end of his fourth jam tart the Terror said: "Of course overseers have a salary."

"Of course they do," said Erebus.

"That settles the matter of pocket-money," said the Terror. "We'll have sixpence a week each."

"Only sixpence?" said Erebus in a tone of the liveliest surprise.

Edgar Jepson

"Well, you see, there are the bicycles. I don't think we can make it more than sixpence. And I tell you what: we shall have to keep accounts. I'll buy an account-book. You're very good at arithmetic—you'll like keeping accounts," said the Terror suavely.

Since her mouth was full of luscious jam tart, Erebus did not feel that it would be delicate at that moment to protest. Therefore on leaving the shop the Terror bought an account-book. His distrust of literature prevented him from paying more than a penny for it. From the stationer's he went to an ironmonger's and bought a saw, a brace, a gimlet, a screw-driver and two gross of screws—his tool-box had long needed refilling. Then they mounted their machines proudly (they had learned to ride on the machines of acquaintances) and rode home. After their visit to the confectioner's they rode rather sluggishly.

They were not hungry, far from it, at the moment; but half-way home the Terror turned out of the main road into the lanes, and they paused at a quiet orchard, in a lovely unguarded spot, and filled the cat-basket on Erebus' bicycle with excellent apples. The tools had been packed into the Terror's basket. They did not disturb the farmer's wife at the busy dinner-hour; the Terror threw the apples over the orchard hedge to Erebus.

As he remembered his bicycle he said dreamily: "I shouldn't wonder if these bicycles didn't pay for themselves in time."

"I said there were orchards out here where they didn't know us," said Erebus, biting into a Ribston pippin.

They reached home in time for lunch and locked away their bicycles in the cow-house. At lunch they were reticent about their triumphs of the morning.

After lunch they went to the cow-house and took measurements. It had long been unoccupied by cows and needed little cleaning. It was quite suitable to their purpose, a brick building with a slate roof and of a size to hold two cows. The measurements made, they went, with an important moneyed air, down to the village carpenter, the only timber merchant in the neighborhood, and bought planks from him. There was some discussion before his idea about the price of planks and that of the Terror were in exact accord; and as he took the money he said, with some ruefulness, that he was a believer in small profits and quick returns. Since immediate delivery was part of the bargain, he forthwith put the planks on a hand-cart and wheeled them up to Colet House. The Twins, eager to be at work, helped him.

For the rest of the day the Terror applied his indisputable constructive genius to the creation of cat-hutches. That evening Erebus wrote his warm letter of thanks to Lady Ryehampton.

The next morning, with a womanly disregard of obligation, Erebus proposed that they should forthwith mount their bicycles and sally forth on a splendid foray. The Terror would not hear of it.

"No," he said firmly. "We're going to get the cats' home finished before we use those bicycles at all. Then nobody can complain."

He lost no time setting to work on it, and worked till it was time to go down to the vicarage for his morning's lessons with the vicar. He set to work again as soon as he returned; he worked all the afternoon; and he saw to it that Erebus worked, too.

In the middle of the afternoon Wiggins came. He had spent a

Edgar Jepson

fruitless hour lying in wait on the common to scalp the Twins as they sallied forth into the world, and then had come to see what had kept them within their borders. He was deeply impressed by the sight of the bicycles, but not greatly surprised: his estimation of the powers of his friends was too high for any of their exploits to surprise him greatly. But he was somewhat aggrieved that they should have obtained their bicycles before he had obtained his. None the less he helped them construct the cats' home with enthusiasm.

For three strenuous days they persisted in their untiring effort. So much sustained carpentering was hard on their hands; many small pieces were chipped out of them. But their spirits never flagged; and by sunset on the third day they had constructed accommodation for thirty cats. It may be that the wooden bars of the hutches were not all of the same breadth, but at any rate they were all of the same thickness: and it would be a slim cat, indeed, that would squirm through them.

At sunset on the third day the exultant trio gazed round the transformed cow-house with shining triumphant eyes; then Erebus said firmly: "What we want now is cats."

CHAPTER IV

AND THE VISIT OF INSPECTION

Cats did not immediately flow in, though the Twins, riding round the countryside on their bicycles, spread the information that they were willing to afford a home to such of those necessary animals as their owners no longer needed. They had, indeed, one offer of a cat suffering from the mange; but the Terror rejected it, saying coldly to its owner that theirs was a home, not a hospital.

The impatient Erebus was somewhat vexed with him for rejecting it: she pointed out that even a mangy cat was a beginning.

Slowly they grew annoyed that the home on which they had lavished such strenuous labor remained empty; and at last the Terror said: "Look here: I'm going to begin with kittens."

"How will you get kittens, if you can't get cats? Everybody likes kittens. It's only when they grow up and stop playing that they don't want them," said Erebus with her coldest scorn.

"I'm going to buy them," said the Terror firmly. "I'm going to give threepence each for kittens that can just lap. We don't want kittens that can't lap. They'd be too much trouble."

"That's a good idea," said Erebus, brightening.

"It'll stop them drowning kittens all right. The only thing I'm not sure about is the accounts."

"You're always bothering about those silly old accounts!" said Erebus sharply.

She resented having had to enter in their penny ledger the items of their expenditure with conspicuous neatness under his critical eye.

"Well, I don't think the kittens ought to go down in the accounts. Aunt Amelia is so used to cats' homes that are given their cats. She's told me all about it: how people write and ask for their cats to be taken in."

"*I* don't want them to go down. It makes all the less accounts to keep," said Erebus readily.

"Well, that's settled," said the Terror cheerfully.

Once more the Twins rode round the countryside, spreading abroad the tidings of their munificent offer of threepence a head for kittens who could just lap.

But kittens did not immediately flow in; and the complaints of the impatient Erebus grew louder and louder. There was no doubt that she loved a grievance; and even more she loved making no secret of that grievance to those about her. Since she could only discuss this grievance with the Terror and Wiggins, they heard enough about it. Indeed, her complaints were at last no small factor in her patient brother's resolve to take action; and he called her and

Wiggins to a council.

He opened the discussion by saying: "We've got to have kittens, or cats. We can't have any pocket-money for 'overseeing' till there's something to overseer."

"And that splendid cats' home we've made stopping empty all the time," said Erebus in her most bitterly aggrieved tone.

"I don't mind that. I'm sick of hearing about it," said the Terror coldly. "But I do want pocket-money; and besides, Aunt Amelia will soon be wanting to know what's happening to the home; and she'll make a fuss if there aren't any cats in it. So we must have cats."

"Well, I tell you what it is: we must take cats. There are cats all over the country; and when we're out bicycling, a good way from home, we could easily pick up one or two at a time and bring them back with us. We ought to be able to get four a day, counting kittens; and in eight days the home would be full and two over."

"And we should be prosecuted for stealing them," said the Terror coldly.

"But they'd be ever so much better off in the home, properly looked after and fed," protested Erebus.

"That wouldn't make any difference. No; it's no good trying to get them that way," said the Terror in a tone of finality.

"Well, they won't come of themselves," said Erebus.

"They would with valerian," said Wiggins.

"Who's Valerian?" said Erebus.

"It isn't a who. It's a drug at the chemist's," said Wiggins. "I've been talking to my father about cats a good deal lately, and he says if you put valerian on a rag and drag it along the ground, cats will follow it for miles."

"Your father seems to know everything—such a lot of useful things as well as higher mathematics," said the Terror.

"That's why he has a European reputation," said Wiggins; and he spurned the earth.

That afternoon the Twins bicycled into Rowington and bought a bottle of the enchanting drug. Just before they reached the village, on their way home, the Terror produced a rag with a piece of string tied to it, poured some valerian on it and trailed it after his bicycle through the village to his garden gate.

The result demonstrated the accuracy of the scientific knowledge of the father of Wiggins. All that evening and far into the night twelve cats fought clamorously round the house of the Dangerfields.

The next day the Terror turned the cats' home into a cat-trap. He cut a hole in the bottom of its door large enough to admit a cat and fitted it with a hanging flap which a cat would readily push open from the outside, but lacked the intelligence to raise from the inside. He was late finishing it, and went from it to his dinner.

They had just come to the end of the simple meal when they heard a ring at the back door; and old Sarah came in to say that Polly Cotteril had come from the village with some kittens. The Twins excused themselves politely to their mother, and hurried to the kitchen to find that Polly had brought no less than five small kittens in a basket.

Forthwith the Terror filled a saucer with milk and applied the lapping test. Four of the kittens lapped the milk somewhat feebly, but they lapped. The fifth would not lap. It only mewed. Therefore the Terror took only four of the kittens, giving Polly a shilling for them. The fifth he returned to her, bidding her bring it back when it could lap.

They took the four kittens down to the cats' home; and since they were so small, they put them in one hutch for warmth, with a saucer of milk to satisfy their hunger during the night.

"Now we've got these kittens, we needn't bother about getting cats," said the Terror as they returned to the house. "And I'm glad it is kittens and not cats. Kittens eat less."

"Then you've had all the trouble of making that little door for nothing," said Erebus.

"It's an emergency exit—like the theaters have—only it's an entrance," said the Terror. "But thank goodness, we've begun at last; now we can have salaries for 'overseeing'."

During the course of the next week they added seven more small kittens to their stock; and it seemed good to the Terror to inform Lady Ryehampton that the home was already constructed and in process of occupation. Accordingly Erebus wrote a letter, by no means devoid of enthusiasm, informing her that it already held eleven inmates, "saved from the awful death of drowning." Lady Ryehampton replied promptly in a spirit of warm gratification that they had been so quick starting it.

But with eleven inmates in the home the Twins presently found themselves grappling earnestly with the food problem and the account-book.

The Terror was not unfitted for financial operations. Till they were six years old the Twins had lived luxuriously at Dangerfield Hall, in Monmouth, with toys beyond the dreams of Alnaschar. Then their father had fallen into the hands of a firm of gambling stock-brokers, had along with them lost nearly all his money, and presently died, leaving Mrs. Dangerfield with a very small income indeed. All the while since his death it had been a hard struggle to make both ends meet; and the Twins had had many a lesson in learning to do without the desires of their hearts.

But their desires were strong; the wits of the Terror were not weak; and taking one month with another the Twins had as much pocket-money as the bulk of the children of the well-to-do. But it did not come in the way of a regular allowance; it had to be obtained by diplomacy or work; and the processes of getting it had given the Terror the liveliest interest in financial matters. He was resolved that the cats' home and the wages of "overseeing" should last as long as possible.

But it soon grew clear to him that, with milk at threepence halfpenny a quart, the kittens would soon drink themselves out of house and home.

He discussed the matter with Erebus and Wiggins; and they agreed with him that milk spelled ruin. But they could see no way of reducing the price of milk; and they were sure that it was the necessary food for growing kittens.

Their faces were somewhat gloomy at the end of the discussion; and a heavy silence had fallen on them. Then of a sudden the face of the Terror brightened; and he said with a touch of triumph in his tone: "I've got it; we'll feed them on skim-milk."

"They feed pigs on skim-milk, not kittens," said Erebus scornfully.

That was indeed the practise at Little Deeping. Butter-making was its chief industry; and the skim-milk went to the pigs.

"If it fattens pigs, it will fatten kittens," said the Terror firmly.

"But how can we get it? They don't sell it about here," said Erebus. "And you know what they are: if Granfeytner didn't sell skim-milk, nobody's going to sell skim-milk to-day."

"Oh, yes: old Stubbs will sell it," said the Terror confidently.

"Old Stubbs! But he hates us worse than any one!" cried Erebus.

"Oh, yes; he doesn't like us. But he's awfully keen on money; every one says so. And he won't care whose money he gets so long as he gets it. Come on; we'll go and talk to him about it," said the Terror.

The Twins went firmly across the common to the house of farmer Stubbs and knocked resolutely. The maid, who was well aware that her master and the Twins were not on friendly terms, admitted them with some hesitation. The Twins had never entered the farmer's house before, though they had often entered his orchard; and they felt slightly uncomfortable. They found the parlor into which they were shown uncommonly musty.

Presently Mr. Stubbs came to them, pulling doubtfully at the Newgate fringe that ran bristling under his chin, with a look of deep suspicion in his small, ferrety, red-rimmed eyes.

Edgar Jepson

Even when he learned that they had come on business, his face did not brighten till the Terror incidentally dropped a sovereign on the floor and talked of cash payments. Then his face shone; he made the admission, cautiously, that he might be induced to sell skim-milk; and then they came to the discussion of prices. Mr. Stubbs wanted to see skim-milk in quarts; the Terror could only see it in pails; and this difference of point of view nearly brought the negotiations to an abrupt end twice. But the Terror's suavity prevented a complete break; and in the end they struck a bargain that he should have as much skim-milk as he required at threepence halfpenny the pailful.

In the course of the next fortnight they admitted twelve more kittens to the home; and the Terror had yet another idea. Milk alone seemed an insufficient diet for them; and he approached the village baker on the matter of stale bread. There were more negotiations; and in the end the Terror made a contract with the baker for a supply of it at nearly his own price. Now he fed the kittens on bread and milk; they throve on it; and it went further than plain milk.

The Twins enjoyed but little leisure. They had been busy filling certain shelves, which they had fixed up above the cat-hutches, with the best apples the more peaceful and sparsely populated parts of the countryside afforded. But what spare time he had the Terror devoted to a great feat of painting. He painted in white letters on a black board:—

LADY RYEHAMPTON'S CATS' HOME

The letters varied somewhat in size, and they were not everything that could be desired in the matter of shape; but both Erebus and Wiggins agreed that it was extraordinarily effective, and that if ever their aunt saw it she would be deeply gratified.

With this final open advertisement of their enterprise ready to be fixed up, they felt that the time had come to take their mother formally into their confidence. She had learned of the formation of the cats' home from old Sarah; and several of her neighbors had talked to her about it, and seemed surprised by her inability to give them details about its ultimate scope and purpose, for it had excited the interest of the neighborhood and was a frequent matter of discussion for fully a week. She had explained to them that she never interfered with the Twins when they were engaged in any harmless employment, and that she was only too pleased that they had found a harmless employment that filled as much of their time as did the cats' home. Moreover, the Terror had told her that they did not wish her to see it till it had been brought to its finished state and was in thorough working order. Therefore she had no idea of its size or of the cost of its construction. Like every one else she supposed it to be a ramshackle affair of makeshifts constructed from old planks and hen-coops.

Moreover she had not learned that the Twins possessed bicycles, for they were judicious in their use. They were careful to sally forth when she was taking her siesta after lunch; they went across the common and came back across the common and their neighbors saw them riding very little.

When at last she was invited to come to see their finished work, she accepted the invitation with becoming delight, and made her inspection of the home with a becoming serious-ness and a growing surprise. She expressed her admiration of its convenience, its cleanliness, and the extensive scale on which it was being run. She agreed with the Terror that to have saved so many kittens from the awful death of drowning was a great work. But she asked no questions, not even how it was that the cats' home was fragrant with the scent of hidden apples. She knew that an explanation, probably of an admirable plausibility, was about to be given her.

Then at the end of her inspection, the Terror said carelessly: "The bicycles are for bringing kittens from a distance, of course."

"What? Are those your bicycles?" cried Mrs. Dangerfield. "But wherever did you get the money from to buy them?"

"Aunt Amelia found the money," said the Terror. "You know she's very keen—tremendously interested in cats' homes. She thinks we are doing a great work, as well as you."

Mrs. Dangerfield's beautiful eyes were very wide open; and she said rather breathlessly: "You got money out of your Aunt Amelia for a cats' home in Little Deeping?"

"Oh, yes," said the Terror carelessly.

Mrs. Dangerfield turned away hastily to hide her working face: she *must* not laugh at their great-aunt before the Twins. She bit her tongue with a firmness that filled her eyes with tears. It was painful; but it enabled her to complete her inspection with the required gravity.

The Terror fixed up the board above the door of the home, and it awoke a fresh interest among their neighbors in their enterprise. Several of them, including the squire and the vicar, made visits of inspection to it; and Wiggins brought his father. All of them expressed an admiration of the institution and of the methods on which it was conducted. To one another they expressed an unfavorable opinion of the intelligence of Lady Ryehampton.

The home was now working quite smoothly; and with a clear

conscience the Twins drew their salary for "overseeing." It provided them with many of the less expensive desires of their hearts. Now and again Erebus, mindful of the fact that they had still a little more than ten pounds left out of the original thirty, urged that it should be raised to a shilling a week. But the Terror would not consent: he said their salaries for "overseeing" would naturally be much higher, and that they would have charged for their work in constructing the home, if it had not been for the bicycles. As it was, they were bound to work off the price of the bicycles. Besides, he added with a philosophical air, six-pence a week for a year was much better than a shilling a week for six months.

Lady Ryehampton was duly informed that the home now contained twenty-three inmates; and the children of Great Deeping, Muttle (probably a corruption of Middle) Deeping, and Little Deeping were informed that for the time being the home was full. Erebus clamored to have its full complement of thirty kittens made up; but the Terror maintained very firmly his contention that twenty-three was quite enough. Everything was working smoothly. Then one evening just before dinner there came a loud ringing at the front-door bell.

It was so loud and so importunate that with one accord the Twins dashed for the door; and Erebus opened it. On the steps stood their Uncle Maurice; and he wore a harried air.

"Why, it's Uncle Maurice!" cried Erebus springing upon him and embracing him warmly.

"It's Uncle Maurice, mother!" cried the Terror.

"It may be your Uncle Maurice, but I can tell you he's by no means sure of it himself! Is it my head or my heels I'm standing on?" said Sir Maurice faintly, and he wiped his burning brow.

On his words there came up the steps the porter of Little Deeping station, laden with wicker baskets. From the baskets came the sound of mewing.

"Whatever is it?" cried Mrs. Dangerfield, kissing her brother.

"Cats for the cats' home!" said Sir Maurice Falconer.

He waved his startled kinsfolk aside while the baskets were ranged in a neat row on the floor of the hall, then he paid the porter, feebly, and shut the door after him with an air of exhaustion. He leaned back against it and said:

"I had a sudden message—Aunt Amelia is going to pay a surprise visit to this inf—this cats' home these little friends are pretending to run for her. I saw that there was no time to lose—there must be a cats' home with cats in it—or she'd cut them both out of her will. I bought cats—all over London—they've been with me ever since—yowling—they yowled in the taxi—all over London—they traveled down as far as Rowington with me and an old gentleman—a high-spirited old gentleman—yowling—not only the cats but the old gentleman, too—and they traveled from Rowington to Little Deeping with me and two maiden ladies—timid maiden ladies!—yowling! But come on: we've got to make a cats' home at once!" And he picked up one of the plaintive baskets with the air of a man desperately resolved to act on the instant or perish.

"But we've got a cats' home—only it's full of kittens," said Erebus gently.

"Good heavens! Do you mean to say I've gone through this nightmare for nothing?" cried Sir Maurice, dropping the basket.

"Oh, no; it was awfully good of you!" said the Terror with swift politeness. "The cats will come in awfully useful."

"They'll make the home look so much more natural. All kittens isn't natural," said Erebus.

"And they'll be such a pleasant surprise for Aunt Amelia. She was only expecting kittens," said the Terror.

"What?" howled Sir Maurice. "Do you mean to say I've parleyed for hours with a high-spirited gentleman and two—two—timid maiden ladies, just to give your Aunt Amelia a pleasant surprise?"

He sank into a chair and wiped his beaded brow feebly. "I ought to have had more confidence in you," he said faintly. "I ought to know your powers by now. And I did. I know well that any people who have dealings with you are likely to get a surprise; but I thought your Aunt Amelia was going to get it; and I've got it myself."

"But you didn't think that we would humbug Aunt Amelia?" said the Terror in a pained tone and with the most virtuous air.

"Gracious, no!" cried Sir Maurice. "I only thought that you might possibly induce her to humbug herself."

The Twins looked at him doubtfully: there seemed to them more in his words than met the ear.

"You must be wanting your dinner dreadfully," said Mrs. Dangerfield. "And I'm afraid there's very little for you. But I'll make you an omelette."

Edgar Jepson

"I can not dine amid this yowling," said Sir Maurice firmly, waving his hand over the vocal baskets. "These animals must be placed out of hearing, or I shan't be able to eat a morsel."

"We'll put them in the cats' home," said the Terror quickly. "I'll just put on a pair of thick gloves. Wiggins' father—he's a higher mathematician, you know, and understands all this kind of thing—says that hydrophobia is very rare among cats. But it's just as well to be careful with these London ones."

"Oh, lord, I never thought of that," said Sir Maurice with a shudder. "I've been risking my life as well!"

The Terror put on the gloves and lighted a lantern. He and Erebus helped carry the cats down to the home; and he put them into hutches. Their uncle was much impressed by the arrangement of the home.

The cats disposed of, Sir Maurice at last recovered his wonted self-possession—a self-possession as admirable as the serenity of the Terror, but not so durable. At dinner he reduced his appreciative kinsfolk to the last exhaustion by his entertaining account of his parleying with his excited fellow travelers. He could now view it with an impartial mind. After dinner he accompanied the Terror to the cats' home and helped him feed the newcomers with scraps. The rest of the evening passed peacefully and pleasantly.

If the Twins had a weakness, it was that their desire for thoroughness sometimes caused them to overdo things; and it was on the way to bed that the brilliant idea flashed into the mind of Erebus.

She stopped short on the stairs, and with an air of inspiration said: "We ought to have more cats."

The Terror stopped short too, pondering the suggestion; then he said: "By Jove, yes. This would be a good time to work that valerian dodge. And it would mean that we should have to use our bicycles again for the good of the home. The more we can say that we've used them for it, the less any one can grumble about them."

"Most cats are shut up now," said Erebus.

"Yes; we must catch the morning cats. They get out quite early—when people start out to work," said the Terror.

Among the possessions of the Twins was an American clock fitted with an alarm. The Terror set it for half past five. At that hour it awoke him with extreme difficulty. He awoke Erebus with extreme difficulty. Five minutes later they were munching bread and butter in the kitchen to stay themselves against the cold of the bitter November morning; then they sallied forth, equipped with rags, string and the bottle of valerian.

They bicycled to Muttle Deeping. There the Terror poured valerian on one of the rags and tied it to the bicycle of Erebus. Forthwith she started to trail it to the cats' home. He rode on to Great Deeping and trailed a rag from there through Little Deeping to the cats' home. When he reached it he found Erebus' bicycle in its corner; and when, after strengthening the trail through the little hanging door with a rag freshly wetted with the drug, he returned to the house, he found that she was already in bed again. He made haste back to bed himself.

It had been their intention to go down to the home before breakfast and put the cats they had attracted to it into hutches. But they slept on till breakfast was ready; and the fragrance of the coffee and bacon lured them straight into the dining-room. After all, as Erebus told the hesitating Terror, there was plenty of time to deal with the new cats, for Aunt Amelia could not reach Little Deeping before eleven o'clock. They could not escape from the home. The Twins therefore devoted their most careful attention to their breakfast with their minds quite at ease.

Then there came a ring at the front door; and still their minds were at ease, for they took it that it was a note or a message from a neighbor. Then Sarah threw open the dining-room door, said "Please, ma'am, it's Lady Ryehampton"; and their Aunt Amelia stood, large, round and formidable, on the threshold. Behind her stood Miss Hendersyde looking very anxious.

There was a heavy frown on Lady Ryehampton's stern face; and when they rose to welcome her, she greeted them with severe stiffness. To Erebus, the instructor of parrots, she gave only one finger.

Then in deep portentous tones she said: "I came down to pay a surprise visit to your cats' home. I always do. It's the only way I can make sure that the poor dear things are receiving proper treatment." The frown on her face grew rhadamanthine. "And last night I saw your Uncle Maurice at the station—he did not see me—with cats, London cats, in baskets. On the labels of two of the baskets I read the names of well-known London cat-dealers. I do not support a cats' home at Little Deeping for London cats bought at London dealers. Why have they been brought here?"

Sir Maurice opened his mouth to explain; but the Terror was before him:

"It was Uncle Maurice's idea," he said. "He didn't think that there ought only to be kittens in a cats' home. We didn't mind ourselves; and of course, if he puts cats in it, he'll have to subscribe to the home. What we have started it for was kittens—to save them from the awful death of drowning. We wrote and told you. And we've saved quite a lot."

His limpid blue eyes were wells of candor.

Lady Ryehampton uttered a short snort; and her eyes flashed.

"Do you mean to tell me that your Uncle Maurice is fond enough of cats to bring them all the way from London to a cats' home at Deeping? He hates cats, and always has!" she said fiercely.

"Of course, I hate cats," said Sir Maurice with cold severity. "But I hate children's being brought up to be careless a great deal more. A cats' home is not a cats' home unless it has cats in it; and you've been encouraging these children to grow up careless by calling a kittens' home a cats' home. If you will interfere in their up-bringing, you have no right to do your best to get them into careless ways."

Taken aback at suddenly finding herself on the defensive Lady Ryehampton blinked at him somewhat owlishly: "That's all very well," she said in a less severe tone. "But is there a kittens' home at all—a kittens' home with kittens in it? That's what I want to know."

"But we wrote and told you how many kittens we had in the cats' home. You don't think we'd deceive you, Aunt Amelia?" said the Terror in a deeply injured tone and with a deeply injured air.

"There! I told you that if he said he had kittens in it, there would be," said Miss Hendersyde with an air of relief.

"Of course there's a cats' home with kittens in it!" said Mrs. Dangerfield with some heat. "The Terror wouldn't lie to you!"

"Hyacinth is incapable of deceit!" cried Sir Maurice splendidly.

The Terror did his best to look incapable of deceit; and it was a very good best.

In some confusion Lady Ryehampton began to stammer: "Well, of c-c-c-course, if there's a c-c-cats' home—but Sir Maurice's senseless interference—"

"Senseless interference! Do you call saving children from careless habits senseless interference?" cried Sir Maurice indignantly.

"You had no business to interfere without consulting me,' said Lady Ryehampton. Then, with a return of suspicion, she said: "But I want to see this cats' home—now!"

"I'll take you at once,' said the Terror quickly, and politely he opened the door.

They all went, Mrs. Dangerfield snatching a hooded cloak, Sir Maurice his hat and coat from pegs in the hall as they went through it. When they came into the paddock their ears became aware of a distant high-pitched din; and the farther they went down it the louder and more horrible grew the din.

Over the broad round face of Lady Ryehampton spread an expression of suspicious bewilderment; Mrs. Dangerfield's beautiful eyes were wide open in an anxious wonder; the piquant face of Erebus was set in a defiant scowl; and Sir Maurice looked almost as anxious as Mrs. Dangerfield. Only the Terror was serene.

"Surely those brutes I brought haven't got out of their cages," said Sir Maurice.

"Oh, no; those must be visiting cats," said the Terror calmly.

"Visiting cats?" said Lady Ryehampton and Sir Maurice together.

"Yes: we encourage the cats about here to come to the home so that if ever they are left homeless they will know where to come," said the Terror, looking at Lady Ryehampton with eyes that were limpid wells of guilelessness.

"Now that's a very clever idea!" she exclaimed. "I must tell the managers of my other homes about it and see whether they can't do it, too. But what are these cats doing?"

"It sounds as if they were quarreling," said the Terror calmly.

It did sound as if they were quarreling; at the door of the home the din was ear-splitting, excruciating, fiendish. It was as if the voices of all the cats in the county were raised in one piercing battle-song.

The Terror bade his kinsfolk stand clear; then he threw open the door—wide. Cats did not come out. . . . A large ball of cats came out, gyrating swiftly in a haze of flying fur. Ten yards from the door it dissolved into its component parts, and some thirty cats tore, yelling, to the four quarters of the heavens.

After that stupendous battle-song the air seemed thick with silence.

Edgar Jepson

The Terror broke it; he said in a tone of doubting sadness: "I sometimes think it sets a bad example to the kittens."

Sir Maurice turned livid in the grip of some powerful emotion. He walked hurriedly round to the back of the home to conceal it from human ken. There with his handkerchief stuffed into his mouth, he leaned against the wall, and shook and rocked and kicked the irresponsive bricks feebly.

But the serene Terror firmly ushered Lady Ryehampton into the home with an air of modest pride. A little dazed, she entered upon a scene of perfect, if highly-scented, peace. Twenty-three kittens and eight cats sat staring earnestly through bars of their hutches in a dead stillness. Their eyes were very bright. By a kindly provision of nature they had been able, in the darkness, to follow the fortunes of that vociferous fray.

In three minutes Lady Ryehampton had forgotten the battle-song. She was charmed, lost in admiration of the home, of the fatness and healthiness of the blinking kittens, the neatness and the cleanliness. She gushed enthusiastic appro-bation. "To think," she cried, "that you have done this yourself! A boy of thirteen!"

"Erebus did quite as much as I did," said the Terror quickly.

"And Wiggins helped a lot. He's a friend of ours," said Erebus no less quickly.

Lady Ryehampton's face softened to Erebus—to Erebus, the instructor of parrots.

Sir Maurice joined them. His eyes were red and moist, as if they had but now been full of tears.

"It's a very creditable piece of work," he said in a tone of warm approval.

Lady Ryehampton looked round the home once more; and her face fell. She said uneasily: "But you must be heavily in debt."

"In debt?" said the Terror. "Oh, no; we couldn't be. Mother would hate us to be in debt."

"I thought—a cats' home—oh, but I *am* glad I brought my check-book with me!" cried Lady Ryehampton.

She could not understand why Sir Maurice uttered a short sharp howl. She did not know that the Terror dug him sharply in the ribs as Erebus kicked him joyfully on the ankle-bone; that they had simultaneously realized that the future of the home, the wages of "overseeing," were secure.

CHAPTER V

AND THE SACRED BIRD

Lady Ryehampton did not easily tear herself away from the home; and the Terror did all he could to foster her interest in it. The crowning effect was the feeding of the kittens, which was indeed a very pretty sight, since twenty-three kittens could not feed together without many pauses to gambol and play. The only thing about the home which was not quite to the liking of Lady Ryehampton was the board over the door. She liked it as an advertisement of her philanthropy; but she did not like its form; she preferred her name in straighter letters, all of them of the same size. At the same time she did not like to hurt the feelings of the Terror by showing lack of appreciation of his handiwork.

Then she had a happy thought, and said: "By the way, I think that the board over the door ought to be uniform—the same as the boards over the entrances of my other cats' homes. The lettering of them is always in gold."

"All right. I'll get some gold paint, and paint them over," said the Terror readily, anxious to humor in every way this dispenser of salaries.

"No, no, I can't give you the trouble of doing it all over

again," said Lady Ryehampton quickly. "I'll have a board made, and painted in London—exactly like the board of my cats' home at Tysleworth—and sent down to you to fix up."

"Thanks very much," said the Terror. "It will save me a great deal of trouble. Painting isn't nearly so easy as it looks."

Lady Ryehampton breathed a sigh of satisfaction. She invited them all to lunch at The Plough, where she had stayed the night; and Mrs. Pittaway racked her brains and strained all the resources of her simple establishment to make the lunch worthy of its giver. As she told her neighbors later, nobody knew what it was to have a lady of title in the house. The Twins enjoyed the lunch very much indeed; and even Erebus was very quiet for two hours after it.

Lady Ryehampton came to tea at Colet House; she paid a last gloating visit to the cats' home, wrote a check for ten pounds payable to the Terror, and in a state of the liveliest satisfaction, took the train to London.

Sir Maurice stayed till a later train, for he had no great desire to travel with Lady Ryehampton. Besides, the question what was to be done with the eight cats he had brought with him, remained to be settled. He felt that he could not saddle the Twins with their care and up-keep, since only his unfounded distrust had brought them to the cats' home. At the same time he could not bring himself to travel with them any more.

They discussed the matter. Erebus was inclined to keep the cats, declaring that it would be so nice to grow their own kittens. The Terror, looking at the question from the cold monetary point of view, wished to be relieved of them. In the end it was decided that Sir Maurice should make terms with one of the dealers from whom he had bought them, and that the Twins should forward them to that dealer.

The next day the Twins discussed what should be done with this unexpected ten pounds which Lady Ryehampton had bestowed on the home. Erebus was for at once increasing their salaries to three shillings a week. The cautious Terror would only raise them to ninepence each. Then, keeping rather more than four pounds for current expenses, he put fifteen pounds in the Post-Office Savings Bank. He thought it a wise thing to do: it prevented any chance of their spending a large sum on some sudden overwhelming impulse.

Then for some time their lives moved in a smooth uneventful groove. The cats were despatched to the London dealer; the neatly painted board came from Lady Ryehampton and was fixed up in the place of the Terror's handiwork; they did their lessons in the morning; they rode out, along with Wiggins who now had his bicycle, in the afternoons.

Then came December: and early in the month they began to consider the important matter of their mother's Christmas present.

One morning they were down at the home, giving the kittens their breakfasts and discussing it gravely. The kittens were indulging in engaging gambols before falling into the sleep of repletion which always followed their meals; but the Twins saw them with unsmiling eyes, for the graver matter wholly filled their minds. They could see their way to saving up seven or eight shillings for that present; and so large a sum must be expended with judgment. It must procure something not only useful but also attractive.

They had discussed at some length the respective advantages and attractions of a hair-brush and a tortoise-shell comb to set in the hair, when Erebus, frowning thoughtfully, said: 'I know what she really wants though."

"What's that?" said the Terror sharply.

"It's one of those fur stoles in the window of Barker's at Rowington," said Erebus. "I heard her sigh when she looked at it. She used to have beautiful furs once—when father was alive. But she sold them—to get things for us, I suppose. Uncle Maurice told me so—at least I got it out of him."

The Terror was frowning thoughtfully, too; and he said in a tone of decision: "How much is that stole?"

"Oh, it's no good thinking about it—it's three guineas," said Erebus quickly.

"That's a mort o' money, as old Stubbs says," said the Terror; and the frown deepened on his brow.

"I wonder if we could get it?" said Erebus, and a faint hopefulness dawned in her eyes as she looked at his pondering face. "I should like to. It must be hard on Mum not to have nice things—much harder than for us, because we've never had them—at least, we had them when we were small, but we never got used to them. So we've forgotten."

"No, we're all right as long as we have useful things," said the Terror, without relaxing his thoughtful frown. "But you're right about Mum—she must be different. I've got to think this out."

"Three guineas is such a lot to think out," said Erebus despondently.

"I thought out thirty pounds not so very long ago," said the Terror firmly. "And if you come to think of it, Mum's stole is really more important than bicycles and a cats' home, though not so useful."

Edgar Jepson

"But it's different—we *had* to have bicycles—you said so," said Erebus eagerly.

"Well, we've got to have this stole," said the Terror in a tone of finality; and the matter settled, his brow smoothed to its wonted serenity.

"But how?" said Erebus eagerly.

"Things will occur to us. They always do," said the Terror with a careless confidence.

They began to put the kittens into their hutches. Half-way through the operation the Terror paused:

"I wonder if we could sell any of these kittens? Does any one ever buy kittens?"

"We did; we gave threepence each for these," said Erebus.

"Ah, but we had to buy something in the way of cats for the home. We should never have bought a kitten but for that. We shouldn't have dreamt of doing such a thing."

"I should buy kittens if I were rich and hadn't got any," said Erebus in a tone of decision.

"You would, would you? That's just what I wanted to know: girls will buy kittens," said the Terror in a tone of satisfaction. "Well, we'll sell these."

"But we can't empty the home," said Erebus.

"We wouldn't. We'd buy fresh ones, just able to lap, for threepence each, and sell these at a shilling. We might make nearly a sovereign that way."

"So we should—a whole sovereign!" cried Erebus; then she added in a somewhat envious tone: "You do think of things."

"I have to. Where should we be, if I didn't?" said the Terror.

"But who are we going to sell them to? Everybody round here has cats."

"Yes, they have," said the Terror, frowning again. "Well, we shall have to sell them somewhere else."

They put the sleepy kittens back in their hutches, and walked back to the house, pondering. The Terror collected the books for his morning's work slowly, still thoughtful.

As he was leaving the house he said: "Look here; the place for us to sell them is Rowington. The people round here sell most of their things at Rowington—butter and eggs and poultry and rabbits."

"And Ellen would sell them for us—in the market," said Erebus quickly.

"Of course she would! You see, you think of things, too!" cried the Terror; and he went off to his lessons with an almost cheerful air.

After lunch they rode to Great Deeping to discuss with Ellen the matter of selling their kittens. She had been their nurse for the first four years of their stay at Colet House; and she had left them to marry a small farmer. She had an affection for them, especially for the Terror; and she had not lost touch with them. She welcomed them warmly, ushered them into her little parlor, brought in a decanter of elderberry wine and a cake. When she had helped them to cake and poured out their wine, the Terror broached the matter that had brought

Edgar Jepson

them to her house.

Ellen's mind ran firmly and unswerving in the groove of butter and eggs and poultry, which she carried every market-day to Rowington in her pony-cart. She laughed consumedly at the Terror's belief that any one would want to buy kittens. But unmoved by her open incredulity, he was very patient with her and persuaded her to try, at any rate, to sell their kittens at her stall in Rowington market. Ellen consented to make the attempt, for she had always found it difficult to resist the Terror when he had set his mind on a thing, and she was eager to oblige him; but she held out no hopes of success.

The Terror came away content, since he had gained his end, and did not share her despondency. Erebus, on the other hand, infected by Ellen's pessimism, rode in a gloomy depression.

Presently her face brightened; and with an air of inspiration she said: "I tell you what: even if we don't sell those kittens, we can always buy the stole. There's all that cats' home money in the bank. We can take as much of it as we want, and pay it back by degrees."

"No, we can't," said the Terror firmly. "We're not going to use that money for anything but the cats' home. I promised Mum I wouldn't. Besides, she'd like the stole ever so much better if we'd really earned it ourselves."

"But we shan't," said Erebus gloomily. "If we sold all the kittens, it will only make twenty-three shillings."

"Then we must find something else to sell," said the Terror with decision.

His mind was running on this line, when a quarter of a mile from Little Deeping they came upon Tom Cobb leaning over a gate surveying a field of mangel-wurzel with vacant amiability.

Tom Cobb was the one villager they respected; and he and they were very good friends. Carping souls often said that Tom Cobb had never done an honest day's work in his life. Yet he was the smartest man in the village, the most neatly dressed, always with money in his pocket.

It was common knowledge that his fortunate state arose from his constitutional disability to observe those admirable laws which have been passed for the protection of the English pheasants from all dangers save the small shot of those who have them fed. Tom Cobb waged war, a war of varying fortunes against the sacred bird. Sometimes for a whole season he would sell the victims of the carnage of the war with never a check to his ardor. In another season some prying gamekeeper would surprise him glutting his thirst for blood and gold, and an infuriated bench of magistrates would fine him. The fine was always paid. Tom Cobb was one of those thrifty souls who lay up money against a rainy day.

He turned at the sound of their coming; and he and the Twins greeted one another with smiles of mutual respect. They rode on a few yards; and then the Terror said, "By Jove!" stopped, slipped off his bicycle, and wheeled it back to the gate. Erebus followed him more slowly.

"I've been wondering if you'd do me a favor, Tom," said the Terror. "I've always wanted to know how to make a snare. I'll give you half-a-crown if you'll teach me."

Tom Cobb's clear blue eyes sparkled at the thought of half-a-crown, but he hesitated. He knew the Twins; he knew that

Edgar Jepson

with them a little knowledge was a dangerous thing—for others. He foresaw trouble for the sacred bird; he foresaw trouble for his natural foes, the gamekeepers. He did not foresee trouble for the Twins; he knew them. And very distinctly he saw half-a-crown.

He grinned and said slowly, "Yes, Master Terror, I'll be very 'appy to teach you 'ow to make a snare."

"Thank you. I'll come around to-morrow afternoon, about two," said the Terror gratefully.

"It *will* be nice to know how to make snares!" cried Erebus happily as they rode on. "I wonder we never thought of it before."

"We didn't want a fur stole before," said the Terror.

The next afternoon Erebus in vain entreated him to take her with him to Tom Cobb's cottage to share the lesson in the art of making snares. But the Terror would not. Often he was indulgent; often he was firm. To-day he was firm.

He returned from his lesson with a serene face, but he said rather sadly: "I've still a lot to learn. But come on: I've got to buy something in Rowington."

They rode swiftly into Rowington, for the next day was market-day, and they had to get the kittens ready for Ellen to sell. At Rowington the Terror bought copper wire at an ironmonger's; and he was very careful to buy it of a certain thickness.

They rode home swiftly, and at once selected six kittens for the experiment. Much to the surprise and disgust of those kittens, they washed them thoroughly in the kitchen. They dried them, and decided to keep them in its warmth till the next morning.

After the washing of the kittens, they betook themselves to the making of snares. Erebus, ever sanguine, supposed that they would make snares at once. The Terror had no such expectation; and it was a long while before he got one at all to his liking.

Remembering Tom Cobb's instructions, he washed it, and then put on gloves before setting it in the hole in the hedge through which the rabbits from the common were wont to enter their garden to eat the cabbages. He was up betimes next morning, found a rabbit in the snare, and thrilled with joy. The fur stole had come within the range of possibility.

Before breakfast they made the toilet of the six chosen kittens, brushing them with the Terror's hair-brush till their fur was of a sleekness it had never known before. Then Erebus adorned the neck of each with a bow of blue ribbon. Knowing the ways of kittens, she sewed on the bows, and sewed them on firmly. It could not be doubted that they looked much finer than ordinary unwashed kittens. Directly after breakfast, the Twins put three in the basket of either of their bicycles, rode over to Rowington and handed them over to Ellen.

They would have liked to stay to see what luck she had with them but they had to return to their lessons. After lunch they made three more snares; and the Terror found that the fingers of Erebus were, if anything, more deft at snare-making than his own.

It was late in the afternoon when they reached Rowington again; and when they came to Ellen's stall, they found to their joy that the basket which had held the six kittens

Edgar Jepson

was empty.

Ellen greeted them with a smile of the liveliest satisfaction, and said: "Well, Master Terror, you were right, and I was wrong. I've sold them kitties—every one—and I've had two more ordered. It was when the ladies from the Hill came marketing that they went."

She opened her purse, took out six shillings, and held them out to the Terror.

"Five," said the Terror. "I must pay you a shilling for selling them. It's what they call commission."

"No, sir; I don't want any commission," said Ellen firmly. "As long as those kitties were there, I sold more butter and eggs and fowls than any one else in the market. I haven't had such a good day not ever before. And I'll be glad to sell as many kitties as you can bring me."

The Terror pressed her to accept the shilling, but she remained firm. The Twins rode joyfully home with six shillings.

That night the Terror set his four snares in the hedge of the garden about the common. He caught three rabbits.

The next morning he was silent and very thoughtful as he helped feed the kittens and change the bay in the hutches.

At last he said rather sadly: "It's sometimes rather awkward being a Dangerfield."

"Why?" said Erebus surprised.

"Those rabbits," said the Terror. "I want to sell them. But it's no good going into Rowington and trying to sell them to a poulterer. Even if he wanted rabbits—which he mightn't—he'd only give me sixpence each for them. But if I were to sell them myself *here*, I could get eightpence, or perhaps ninepence each for them. But, you see, a Dangerfield can't go about selling things. Uncle Maurice said I had the makings of a millionaire in me, but a Dangerfield couldn't go into business. It's the family tradition not to. That's what he said."

"Perhaps he was only rotting," said Erebus hopefully.

"No, he wasn't. I asked Mum, and she said it was the family tradition, too. I expect that's why we're all so hard up."

"But the squire sells things," said Erebus quickly. "And you can't say he isn't a gentleman, though the Anstruthers aren't so old as the Dangerfields."

"Of course, he does. He sells some of his game," said the Terror, in a tone of great relief. "Game must be all right, and we can easily count rabbits as game."

Forthwith he proceeded to count rabbits as game; they put the four they had caught into the baskets of their bicycles and rode out on a tour of the neighborhood. The Terror went to the back doors of their well-to-do neighbors and offered his rabbits to their cooks with the gratifying result that in less than an hour he had sold all four of them at eightpence each.

They rode home in triumph: the fur stole was moving toward them. They had already eight shillings and eightpence out of the sixty-three shillings.

It was sometimes said of the Twins by the carping that they never knew when to stop; but in this case it was not their fault that they went on. It was the fault of the rabbit market.

At the fifteenth rabbit, when they had but eighteen shillings and eightpence toward the stole, the bottom fell out of it. For the time the desire of Little Deeping to eat rabbits was sated.

It was also the fault of the insidious cook of Mrs. Blenkinsop, who, after refusing to buy the fifteenth rabbit, said: "Now, if you was to bring me a nice fat pheasant twice a week, it would be a very different thing, Master Dangerfield."

The Terror looked at her thoughtfully; then he said: "And how much would you pay for pheasants?"

The cook made a silent appeal to those processes of mental arithmetic she had learned in her village school, saw her way to a profit of threepence, perhaps ninepence, on each bird, and said: "Two and threepence each, sir."

The Terror looked at her again thoughtfully, considering her offer. He saw her profit of threepence, perhaps ninepence, and said: "All right, I'll bring you two or three a week. But you'll have to pay cash."

"Oh, yes, sir. Of course, sir," said the cook.

"Do you know any one else who'd buy pheasants?" he said.

"Well, there's Mr. Carrington's cook," said the cook slowly. "She has the management of the housekeeping money like I do. I think she might buy pheasants from you. Mr. Carrington's very partial to game."

"Right," said the Terror. "And thank you for telling me."

He rode straight to the house of Mr. Carrington, and broached the matter to his cook, to whom he had already sold rabbits. He made a direct offer to her of two pheasants a week at two and threepence each. After a vain attempt to beat him down to two shillings, she accepted it.

He rode home in a pleasant glow of triumph: the snares which caught rabbits would catch pheasants. At first he was for catching those pheasants by himself. Snaring rabbits was a harmless enterprise; snaring pheasants was poaching; and poaching was not a girl's work. Then he came to the conclusion that he would need the help of Erebus and must tell her.

When he revealed to her this vision of a new Eldorado, she said: "But where are you going to get pheasants from?"

"Woods," said the Terror, embracing the horizon in a sweeping gesture.

Erebus looked round the horizon with greedy eyes; they sparkled fiercely.

"The only thing is, we don't know nearly enough about snaring pheasants. And I don't like to ask Tom Cobb: he might talk about it; and that wouldn't do at all," said the Terror.

"But there's nobody else to ask."

"I don't know about that. There's Wiggins' father. He knows a lot of useful things besides higher mathematics. The only thing is, we must do it in such a way that he doesn't see we're trying to get anything out of him."

"Well, I should think we could do that. He's really quite simple," said Erebus.

"As long as *you* understand what I'm driving at," said the Terror.

That evening they prepared eight more kittens for sale at Rowington market, and carried them into Rowington directly after breakfast next morning. Ellen told them, with some indignation, that two rival poultry-sellers had both brought three kittens to sell. The Twins at once went to inspect them, and came back with the cheering assurance that those kittens were not a patch on those she was selling. They were right, for Ellen sold all the eight before a rival sold one; and the joyful Twins carried home eight more shillings toward the stole.

On the next three afternoons they rode forth with the intention of coming upon Mr. Carrington by seeming accident; but it was not till the third afternoon that they came upon him and Wiggins, walking briskly, about three miles from Little Deeping.

The Twins, as a rule, were wont to shun Mr. Carrington. They had a great respect for his attainments, but a much greater for his humor. In Erebus, this respect often took the form of wriggling in his presence. She did not know what he might say about her next. He was, therefore, somewhat surprised when they slipped off their bicycles and joined him. He wondered what they wanted.

Apparently, they were merely in a gregarious mood, yearning for the society of their fellow creatures; but in about three minutes the talk was running on pheasants. Mr. Carrington did not like pheasants, except from the point of view of eating; and he dwelt at length on the devastation the sacred bird was working in the English countryside: villages were being emptied and let fall to ruin that it might live undisturbed; the song-birds were being killed off to give it the woods to itself.

It seemed but a natural step from the pheasant to the poacher; he was not aware that he took it at the prompting of the Terror; and he bewailed the degeneracy of the British rustic, his slow reversion to the type of neolithic man, owing to the fact that the towns drained the villages of all the intelligent. The skilful poacher who harried the sacred bird was fast becoming extinct.

Then, at last, he came to the important matter of the wiles of the poacher; and the thirsty ears of the Terror drank in his golden words. He discussed the methods of the gang of poachers and the single poacher with intelligent relish and more sympathy than was perhaps wise to display in the presence of the young. The Terror came from that talk with a firm belief in the efficacy of raisins.

The next afternoon the Twins rode into Rowington and bought a pound of raisins at the leading grocer's. They might well have bought them at Little Deeping, encouraging local enterprise; but they thought Rowington safer. They always took every possible precaution at the beginning of an enterprise. They did not ride straight home. Three miles out of Rowington was a small clump of trees on a hill. At the foot of the hill, a hundred yards below the clump, lay Great Deeping wood, acre upon acre. It had lately passed, along with the rest of the Great Deeping estate, into the hands of Mr. D'Arcy Rosenheimer, a pudding-faced, but stanch young Briton of the old Pomeranian strain. He was not loved in the county, even by landed proprietors of less modern stocks, for, though he cherished the laudable ambition of having the finest pheasant shoot in England, and was on the way to realize it, he did not invite his neighbors to help shoot them. His friends came wholly from The Polite World which so adorns the illustrated weeklies.

Edgar Jepson

It was in the deep December dusk that the Twins' came to the clump on the hill. The Terror lifted their bicycles over the gate and set them behind the hedge. He removed the pound of raisins from his bicycle basket to his pocket, and leaving Erebus to keep watch, he stole down the hedge to the clump, crawled through a gap into it, and walked through it. One pheasant scuttled out of it, down the hedgerow to the wood below. The occurrence pleased him. He crawled out of the clump on the farther side, and proceeded to lay a train of raisins down the ditch of the hedge to the wood. He did not lay it right down to the wood lest some inquisitive game-keeper might espy it. Then he returned with fine, red Indian caution to Erebus. They rode home well content.

Next evening, with another bag of raisins, they sought the clump again. Again the Terror laid a trail of raisins along the ditch from the wood to the clump. But this evening he set a snare in the hedge of the clump. Just above the end of the ditch. Later he took from that snare a plump but sacred bird. Later still he sold it to the cook of Mrs. Blenkinsop for two and threepence.

CHAPTER VI

AND THE LANDED PROPRIETOR

On reaching home the Terror displayed the two shillings and threepence to Erebus with an unusual air of triumph; as a rule he showed himself serenely unmoved alike in victory and defeat.

"That's all right," said Erebus cheerfully. "That makes—that makes twenty-eight and eleven-pence. We *are* getting on."

"Yes; it's twenty-eight and eleven-pence now," said the Terror quickly. "But you don't seem to see that when we've got the stole for Mum these pheasants will still be going on."

"Of course they will!" cried Erebus; and her eyes shone very brightly indeed at the joyful thought.

The next day the Terror obtained some sandwiches from Sarah after breakfast; and as soon as his lessons were over he rode hard to the clump above Great Deeping wood. He reached it at the hour when gamekeepers are at their dinner, and was able to make a thorough examination of it. He found it full of pheasant runs, and chose the two likeliest places for his snares. He did not set them then and there; a keeper on his afternoon round might see them. He came again in the evening with Erebus, laid trails of raisins and set them then. Later he sold a pheasant to the cook of Mrs. Blenkinsop and one to the cook of Mr. Carrington.

During the next fortnight they sold eight more pheasants and eight more kittens. They found themselves in the happy position of needing only six shillings more to make up the price of the fur stole.

But it had been impossible for the Twins to remain content with the clump of trees above Great Deeping wood. They had laid a trail of raisins and set a snare in the wood itself, in the nearest corner of it on the valley road which divides the wood into two nearly equal parts.

On the next afternoon they had ridden into Rowington with Wiggins; and since the roads were heavy they did not go back the shortest way over Great Deeping hill, but took the longer level road along the valley. The afternoon was still young, and for December, uncommonly clear and bright. But as they rode through the wood, the Terror decided that instead of returning to it in the favoring dusk he might as well examine the snare in the corner now, and save himself another journey. It was a risk no experienced poacher would have taken; but old heads, alas! do not grow on young shoulders.

He dismounted about the middle of the wood, informed the other two of his purpose (to the surprise of Wiggins who had not been informed of his friends' latest exploits) and made his dispositions. When they came to the corner of the wood, Erebus rode on up the road to keep a lookout ahead. The Terror slipped off his bicycle, and so did Wiggins. Wiggins held the two bicycles. The Terror listened. The wood was very still in its winter silence. He slipped through the hedge into it, and presently came back bringing with him a very nice young pheasant indeed. He put it into the basket of his bicycle, and mounted.

They had barely started when a keeper sprang out of the hedge, thirty yards ahead, and came running toward them, shouting in a very daunting fashion as he came. There was neither time nor room to turn. They rode on; and the keeper made for the Terror. The Terror swerved; and the keeper swerved. Wiggins ran bang into the keeper; and they came to the ground together as the Terror shot ahead, pedaling as hard as he could.

He caught up Erebus, and his cry of "Keeper!" set her racing beside him; but both of them kept looking back for Wiggins; and presently, when no Wiggins appeared, with one accord they slowed down, stopped and dismounted.

"The keeper's got him. This is a mess!" said the Terror, who was panting a little from their spurt.

"If only it had been one of us!" cried Erebus. "Whatever are we to do?"

"If that beastly keeper hadn't seen me with the pheasant, I'd get Wiggins away, somehow," said the Terror. "But, as it is, it's me they really want; and I'd get fined to a dead certainty. Come on, let's go back and see what's happened to him. You scout on ahead. Nobody knows you're in it."

"All right," said Erebus; and she mounted briskly.

She rode back through the wood slowly, her keen eyes straining for a sign of an ambush. The Terror followed her at a distance of sixty yards, ready to jump off, turn his machine, and fly should she give the alarm. They got no sight of Wiggins till they came, just beyond the end of the wood, to the lodges of Great Deeping Park; then, half-way up the drive, they saw the keeper and his prey. The keeper held Wiggins with his left hand and wheeled the captured bicycle with his right. The Twins dismounted. Even at that distance they could see the deep dejection of their friend.

"There's not really any reason for him to be frightened. He was never in the wood at all; and he never touched the pheasant," said the Terror.

"What does that matter? He *will* be frightened out of his life; he's so young," cried Erebus in a tone of acute distress, gazing after their receding friend with very anxious eyes. "He's not like us; he won't cheek the keeper all the way like we should."

"Oh, Wiggins has plenty of pluck," said the Terror in a reassuring tone.

"But he won't understand he's all right. He's only ten. And there's no saying how that beastly foreigner who shoots nightingales will bully him," cried Erebus with unabated anxiety.

This was her womanly irrational conception of a Pomeranian Briton.

"Well, the sooner we go and fetch his father the sooner he'll be out of it," said the Terror, making as if to mount his bicycle.

"No, no! That won't do at all!" cried Erebus fiercely. "We've got to rescue him now—at once. We got him into the mess; and we've got to get him out of it. You've got to find a way."

"It's all very well," said the Terror, frowning deeply; and he took off his cap to wrestle more manfully with the problem.

Erebus faced him, frowning even more deeply.

Never had the Twins been so hopelessly at a loss.

Then the Terror said in his gloomiest tone: "I can't see what we can do."

"Oh, I'm going to get him out of it somehow!" cried Erebus in a furious desperation.

With that she mounted her bicycle and rode swiftly up the drive.

The Terror mounted, started after her, and stopped at the end of fifty yards. It had occurred to him that, after all, he was the only poacher of the three, the only one in real danger. As he leaned on his machine, watching his vanishing sister, he ground his teeth. For all his natural serenity, inaction was in the highest degree repugnant to him.

Erebus reached Great Deeping Court but a few minutes after Wiggins and the keeper. She was about to ride on round the house, thinking that the keeper would, as befitted his station, enter it by the back door, when she saw Wiggins' bicycle standing against one of the pillars of the great porch. In a natural elation at having captured a poacher, and eager to display his prize without delay, the keeper had gone straight into the great hall.

Erebus dismounted and stood considering for perhaps half a minute; then she moved Wiggins' bicycle so that it was right to his hand if he came out, set her own bicycle against another of the pillars, but out of sight lest he should take it by mistake, walked up the steps, hammered the knocker firmly, and rang the bell. The moment the door opened she stepped quickly past the footman into the hall. The keeper sat on a chair facing her, and on a chair beside him sat Wiggins looking white and woebegone.

Erebus gazed at them with angry sparkling eyes, then she said sharply: "What are you doing with my little brother?"

She adopted Wiggins with this suddenness in order to strengthen her position.

The keeper opened his eyes in some surprise at her uncompromising tone, but he said triumphantly:

"I caught 'im poachin'—"

"Stand up! What do you mean by speaking to me sitting down?" cried Erebus in her most imperative tone.

The keeper stood up with uncommon quickness and a sudden sheepish air: "'E was poachin'," he said sulkily.

"He was not! A little boy like that!" cried Erebus scornfully.

"Anyways, 'e was aidin' an' abettin', an' I've brought 'im to Mr. D'Arcy Rosynimer an' it's for 'im to say," said the keeper stubbornly.

There came a faint click from the beautiful lips of Erebus, the gentle click by which the Twins called each other to attention. At the sound Wiggins, his face faintly flushed with hope, braced himself. Erebus measured the distance with the eye of an expert, just as there came into the farther end of the hall that large, flabby, pudding-faced young Pomeranian Briton, Mr. D'Arcy Rosenheimer.

"Where's the boacher?" he roared in an eager, angry voice, reverting in his emotion to the ancestral "b."

As the keeper turned to him Erebus sprang to the door and threw it wide.

"Bolt, Wiggins!" she cried.

Wiggins bolted for the door; the keeper grabbed at him and missed; the footman grabbed, and grabbed the interposing Erebus. She slammed the door behind the vanished Wiggins.

Mr. D'Arcy Rosenheimer dashed heavily down the hall with a thick howl. Erebus set her back against the door. He caught her by the left arm to sling her out of the way. It was a silly arm to choose, for she caught him a slap on his truly Pomeranian expanse of cheek with the full swing of her right, a slap that rang through the great hall like the crack of a whip-lash. Mr. D'Arcy Rosenheimer was large but tender. He howled again, and thumped at Erebus with big flabby fists. She caught the first blow on an uncommonly acute elbow. The second never fell, for the footman caught him by the collar and swung him round.

"It's not for the likes of you to 'it Henglish young ladies!" he cried with patriotic indignation.

Mr. D'Arcy Rosenheimer gasped and gurgled; then he howled furiously, "Ged out of my house! Now—at once—ged out!"

"And pleased I shall be to go—when I've bin paid my wages. It's a month to-morrow since I gave notice, anyhow. I've had enough of furriners," said the footman with cold exultation.

"Go—go—ged oud!" roared Mr. D'Arcy Rosenheimer.

"When I've bin paid my wages," said the footman coldly.

Erebus waited to hear no more. She turned the latch, slipped through the door, and slammed it behind her. To her dismay she saw a big motorcar coming round the corner of the house. She mounted quickly and raced down the drive. Wiggins was already out of sight.

Just outside the lodge gates she found the Terror waiting for her.

"I've sent Wiggins on!" he shouted as she passed.

"Come on! Come on!" she shrieked back. "The beastly foreigner's got a motor-car!"

He caught her up in a quarter of a mile; and she told him that the car had been ready to start. They caught up Wiggins a mile and a half down the road; and all three of them sat down to ride all they knew. They were fully eight miles from home, and the car could go three miles to their one on that good road. The Twins alone would have made a longer race of it; but the pace was set by the weaker Wiggins. They had gone little more than three miles when they heard the honk of the car as it came rapidly round a corner perhaps half a mile behind them.

"Go on, Terror!" cried Erebus. "You're the one that matters! You did the poaching! I'll look after Wiggins! He'll be all right with me."

For perhaps fifty yards the Terror hesitated; then the wisdom of the advice sank in, and he shot ahead. Erebus kept behind Wiggins; and they rode on. The car was overhauling them rapidly, but not so rapidly as it would have done had not Mr. D'Arcy Rosenheimer, who lacked the courage of his famous grenadier ancestors, been in it. He was howling at his straining chauffeur to go slower.

Nevertheless at the end of a mile and a half the car was less than fifty yards behind them; and then a figure came into sight swinging briskly along.

"It's your father!" gasped Erebus.

It was, indeed, the higher mathematician.

As they reached him, they flung themselves off their bicycles; and Erebus cried: "Wiggins hasn't been poaching at all! It was the Terror!"

"Was it, indeed?" said Mr. Carrington calmly.

On his words the car was on them; and as it came to a dead stop Mr. D'Arcy Rosenheimer tumbled clumsily out of it.

"I've got you, you liddle devil!" he bellowed triumphantly, but quite incorrectly; and he rushed at Wiggins who stepped discreetly behind his father.

"What's the matter?" said Mr. Carrington.

The excited young Pomeranian Briton, taking in his age and size at a single glance, shoved him aside with splendid violence. Mr. Carrington seemed to step lightly backward and forward in one movement; his left arm shot out; and there befell Mr. D'Arcy Rosenheimer what, in the technical terms affected by the fancy, is described as "an uppercut on the point which put him to sleep." He fell as falls a sack of potatoes, and lay like a log.

The keeper had just disengaged himself from the car and

hurried forward.

"Do you want some too, my good man?" said Mr. Carrington in his most agreeable tone, keeping his guard rather low.

The keeper stopped short and looked down, with a satisfaction he made no effort to hide, at the body of his stricken employer which lay between them.

"I can't say as I do, sir," he said civilly; and he backed away.

"Then perhaps you'll be good enough to tell me the name of this hulking young blackguard who assaults quiet elderly gentlemen, taking constitutionals, in this most unprovoked and wanton fashion," said the higher mathematician in the same agreeable tone.

"Assaults?—'Im assault?—Yes, sir; it's Mr. D'Arcy Rosenheimer, of Great Deeping Court, sir," said the keeper respectfully.

"Then tell Mr. D'Arcy Rosenheimer, when he recovers the few wits he looks to have, with my compliments, that he will some time this evening be summoned for assault. Good afternoon," said Mr. Carrington, and he turned on his heel.

The keeper and the chauffeur stooped over the body of their young employer. Mr. Carrington did not so much as turn his head. He put his walking-stick under his arm, and rubbed the knuckles of his left hand with rueful tenderness. None the less he looked pleased; it was gratifying to a slight man of his sedentary habit to have knocked down such a large, round Pomeranian Briton with such exquisite neatness. Wheeling their bicycles, Erebus and Wiggins walked beside him with a proud air. They felt that they shone with his reflected glory. It was a delightful sensation.

They had gone some forty yards, when Erebus said in a hushed, awed, yet gratified tone: "Have you killed him, Mr. Carrington?"

"No, my child. I am not a pork-butcher," said Mr. Carrington amiably.

"He *looked* as if he was dead," said Erebus; and there was a faint ring of disappointment in her tone.

"In a short time the young man will come to himself; and let us hope that it will be a better and wiser self," said Mr. Carrington. "But what was it all about? What did that truculent young ruffian want with Rupert?"

Erebus paused, looking earnestly round to the horizon for inspiration; then she dashed at the awkward subject with commendable glibness: "It was a pheasant in Great Deeping wood," she said. "The Terror found it, I suppose. I had gone on, and I didn't see that part. But it was Wiggins the keeper caught. Of course—"

"I beg your pardon; but I should like that point a little clearer," broke in Mr. Carrington. "Had you ridden on too, Rupert? Or did you see what happened?"

"Oh, yes; I was there," said Wiggins readily. "And the Terror found the pheasant in the wood and put it in his bicycle basket. And we had just got on our bicycles when the keeper came out of the wood, and I ran into him; and he collared me and took me up to the Court. I wasn't really frightened—at least, not much."

"The keeper had no right to touch him," Erebus broke in glibly. "Wiggins never touched the pheasant; he didn't even go into the wood; and when I went into the hall, the hall of the Court, I found him and the keeper sitting there, and I let Wiggins out, of course, and then that horrid Mr. D'Arcy Rosenheimer who shoots nightingales, caught hold of me by the arm ever so roughly, and I slapped him just once. I should think that the mark is still there "—her speed of speech slackened to a slower vengeful gratification and then quickened again—"and he began to thump me and the footman interfered, and I came away, and they came after us in the car, and you saw what happened—at least you did it."

She stopped somewhat breathless.

"Lucidity itself," said Mr. Carrington. "But let us have the matter of the pheasant clear. Was the Terror exploring the wood on the chance of finding a pheasant, or had he reason to expect that a pheasant would be there ready to be brought home?"

Erebus blushed faintly, looked round the horizon somewhat aimlessly, and said, "Well, there was a snare, you know."

Mr. Carrington chuckled and said: "I thought so. I thought we should come to that snare in time. Did you know there was a snare, Rupert?"

"Oh, no, he didn't know anything about it!" Erebus broke in quickly. "We should never have thought of letting him into anything so dangerous! He's so young!"

"I shall be eleven in a fortnight!" said Wiggins with some heat.

"You see, we wanted a fur stole at Barker's in Rowington for a Christmas present for mother; and pheasants were the only way we could think of getting it," said Erebus in a confidential tone.

"Light! Light at last!" cried Mr. Carrington; and he laughed gently. "Well, every one has been assaulted except the poacher; exquisitely Pomeranian! But it's just as well that they have, or that ingenious brother of yours would be in a fine mess. As it is, I think we can go on teaching our young Pomeranian not to be so high-spirited." He chuckled again.

He walked on briskly; and on the way to Little Deeping, he drew from Erebus the full story of their poaching. When they reached the village he did not go to his own house, but stopped at the garden gate of Mr. Tupping, the lawyer who had sold his practise at Rowington and had retired to Little Deeping. At his gate Mr. Carrington bade Erebus good afternoon and told her to tell the Terror not to thrust himself on the notice of any of Mr. D'Arcy Rosenheimer's keepers who might be sent out to hunt for the real culprit. He would better keep quiet.

Erebus mounted her bicycle and rode quickly home. She found the Terror in the cats' home, awaiting her impatiently.

"Well, did Wiggins get away all right?" he cried. "I passed Mr. Carrington; and I thought he'd see that they didn't carry him off again."

Erebus told him in terms of the warmest admiration how firmly Mr. Carrington had dealt with the Pomeranian foe.

"By Jove! That was ripping! I do wish I'd been there!" said the Terror. "He only hit him once, you say?"

"Only once. And he told me to tell you to lie low in case Mr. Rosenheimer's keepers are out hunting for you," said Erebus.

"I am lying low," said the Terror. "And I've got rid of that pheasant. I sold it to Mr. Carrington's cook as I came through the village. I thought it was better out of the way."

"Then that's all right. We only want about another half-crown," said Erebus.

Mr. Carrington found Mr. Tupping at home; and he could not have gone to a better man, for though the lawyer had given up active practise, he still retained the work of a few old clients in whom he took a friendly interest; and among them was Mrs. Dangerfield.

He was eager to prevent the Terror from being prosecuted for poaching not only because the scandal would annoy her deeply but also because she could so ill afford the expense of the case. He readily fell in with the view of Mr. Carrington that they had better take the offensive, and that the violent behavior of Mr. D'Arcy Rosenheimer had given them the weapons.

The result of their council was that not later than seven o'clock that evening Mr. D'Arcy Rosenheimer was served by the constable of Little Deeping with a summons for an assault on Violet Anastasia Dangerfield, and with another summons for an assault on Bertram Carrington, F. R. S.; and in the course of the next twenty minutes his keeper was served with a summons for an assault on Rupert Carrington.

Though on recovering consciousness he had sent the keeper to scour the neighborhood for Wiggins and the Terror, Mr. D'Arcy Rosenheimer was in a chastened shaken mood, owing to the fact that he had been "put to sleep by an uppercut on the point." He made haste to despatch a car into Rowington to bring the lawyer who managed his local business.

The lawyer knew his client's unpopularity in the county, and advised him earnestly to try to hush these matters up. He declared that however Pomeranian one might be by extraction and in spirit, no bench of English magistrates would take a favorable view of an assault by a big young man on a middle-aged higher mathematician of European reputation, or on Miss Violet Anastasia Dangerfield, aged thirteen, gallantly rescuing that higher mathematician's little boy from wrongful arrest and detention.

Mr. D'Arcy Rosenheimer held his aching head with both hands, protested that they had done all the effective assaulting, and protested his devotion to the sacred bird beloved of the English magistracy. But he perceived clearly enough that he had let that devotion carry him too far, and that a Bench which never profited by it, so far as to shoot the particular sacred birds on which it was lavished, would not be deeply touched by it. Therefore he instructed the lawyer to use every effort to settle the matter out of court.

The lawyer dined with him lavishly, and then had, himself driven over to Little Deeping in the car, to Mr. Carrington's house. He found Mr. Carrington uncommonly bitter against his client; and he did his best to placate him by urging that the assault had been met with a promptitude which had robbed it of its violence, and that he could well afford to be generous to a man whom he had so neatly put to sleep with an uppercut on the point.

Mr. Carrington held out for a while; but in the background, behind the more prominent figures in the affair, lurked the Terror with a veritable poached pheasant; and at last he made terms. The summonses should be withdrawn on condition that nothing more was heard about that poached pheasant and that Mr. D'Arcy Rosenheimer contributed fifty guineas to the funds of the Deeping Cottage Hospital. The lawyer accepted the terms readily; and his client made no objection to complying with them.

The matter was at an end by noon of the next day; and Mr. Carrington sent for the Terror and talked to him very seriously about this poaching. He did not profess to consider it an enormity; he dwelt at length on the extreme annoyance his mother would feel if he were caught and prosecuted. In the end he gave him the choice of giving his word to snare no more pheasants, or of having his mother informed that he was poaching. The Terror gave his word to snare no more pheasants the more readily since if Mrs. Dangerfield were informed of his poaching, she would forbid him to set another snare for anything. Besides, he had been somewhat shaken by his narrow escape the day before. Only he pointed out that he could not be quite sure of never snaring a pheasant, for pheasants went everywhere. Mr. Carrington admitted this fact and said that it would be enough if he refrained from setting his snares on ground sacred to the sacred bird. If pheasants wandered into them on unpreserved ground, it was their own fault. Thanks therefore to the firmness of her friends Mrs. Dangerfield never learned of the Terror's narrow escape.

The Twins bore the loss of income from the sacred bird with even minds, since the sum needed for the fur stole was so nearly complete. They turned their attention to the habits of the hare, and snared one in the hedge of the farthest meadow of farmer Stubbs. Mrs. Blenkinsop's cook paid them half-a-crown for it; and the three guineas were complete.

Though it wanted a full week to Christmas, the Terror lost no time making the purchase. As he told Erebus, they would get the choice of more stoles if they bought it before the Christmas rush. Accordingly on the afternoon after the sale of the hare they rode into Rowington to buy it.

It was an uncommonly cold afternoon, for a bitter east wind was blowing hard; and when they dismounted at the door of Barker's shop, Erebus gazed wistfully across the road at the appetizing window of Springer, the confectioner, and said sadly:

"It's a pity it isn't Saturday and we had our 'overseeing' salary. We might have gone to Springer's and had a jolly good blow-out for once."

The Terror gazed at Springer's window thoughtfully, and said: "Yes, it is a pity. We ought to have remembered it was Christmas-time and paid ourselves in advance."

He followed Erebus into the shop with a thoughtful air, and seemed somewhat absent-minded during her examination of the stoles. She was very thorough in it; and both of them were nearly sure that she had chosen the very best of them. The girl who was serving them made out the bill; and the Terror drew the little bag which held the three guineas (since it was all in silver they had been able to find no purse of a capacity to hold it), emptied its contents on the counter, and counted them slowly.

He had nearly finished, and the girl had nearly wrapped up the stole when a flash of inspiration brightened his face; and he said firmly: "I shall want five per cent. discount for cash."

"Oh, we don't do that sort of thing here," said the girl quickly. "This is such an old-established establishment."

"I can't help that. I must have discount for cash," said the Terror yet more firmly.

The girl hesitated; then she called Mr. Barker who, acting as his own shop-walker, was strolling up and down with great dignity. Mr. Barker came and she put the matter to him.

"Oh, no, sir; I'm afraid we couldn't think of it. Barker's is too old established a house to connive at these sharp modern ways of doing business," said Mr. Barker with a very impressive air.

The Terror looked at him with a cold thoughtful eye: "All right," he said. "You can put the stole down to me—Master Hyacinth Dangerfield, Colet House, Little Deeping."

He began to shovel the money back into the bag.

An expression of deep pain spread over the mobile face of Mr. Barker as the coins began to disappear; and he said quickly: "I'm afraid we can't do that, sir. Our terms are cash—strictly cash."

"Oh, no, they're not. My mother has had an account here for the last six years," said the Terror icily; and the last of the coins went into the bag.

Mr. Barker held out a quivering hand, and with an air and in a tone of warm geniality he cried: "Oh, that alters the case altogether! In the case of the son of an old customer like Mrs. Dangerfield we're delighted to deduct five per cent. discount for cash—delighted. Make out the bill for three pounds, Miss Perkins."

Miss Perkins made out the bill for three pounds; and Erebus bore away the stole tenderly.

As the triumphant Terror came out of the shop, he jingled the brave three shillings discount in his pocket and said: "Now for Springer's!"

CHAPTER VII

AND PRINGLE'S POND

Mrs. Dangerfield was indeed delighted with the stole, for she had an almost extravagant fondness for furs; and it was long since she had had any. She wondered how the Twins had saved and collected the money it had cost; she knew that it had not been drawn from the cats' home fund, since the Terror had promised her that none of that money should be diverted from its proper purpose; and she was the more grateful to them for the thought and labor they must have devoted to acquiring it. On the whole she thought it wiser not to inquire how the money had been raised.

The Twins, as always, enjoyed an exceedingly pleasant Christmas. It was the one week in the year when Little Deeping flung off its quietude and gently rollicked. There was a dearth of children, young men and maidens among their Little Deeping friends; and the Twins and Wiggins were in request as the lighter element in the Christmas gatherings. Thanks to the Terror, the three of them took this brightening function with considerable seriousness: each of them learned by heart a humorous piece of literature, generally verse, for reciting; and they performed two charades in a very painstaking fashion. They had but little dramatic talent; but they derived a certain grave satisfaction from the discharge of this enlivening social duty; and their efforts were always well received.

It was, as usual, a green and muggy Christmas. The weather broke about the middle of January; and there came hard frosts and a heavy snow-storm. The Twins made a glorious forty-foot slide on the common in front of Colet House; and they constructed also an excellent toboggan on which they rushed down the hill into the village street. These were but light pleasures. They watched the ponds with the most careful interest; eager, should they bear, not to miss an hour's skating. Wiggins shared their pleasures and their interest; and Mr. Carrington, meeting the Terror on his way to his lessons at the vicarage, drew from him a promise that he would not let his ardent son take any risk whatever.

The ice thickened slowly on the ponds; then came another hard frost; and the Twins made up their minds that it must surely bear. They ate their breakfast in a great excitement; and as the Terror gathered together his books for his morning's work they made their plans.

He had strapped his books together; and as he caught up one of the two pairs of brightly polished skates that lay on the table, he said: "Then that's settled. I'll meet you at Pringle's pond as soon after half past twelve as I can get there; but you'd better not go on it before I come."

"Oh, it'll bear all right; it nearly bore yesterday," said Erebus impatiently.

"Well, Wiggins isn't to go on it before I come. You'll do as you like of course—as usual—and if you fall in, it'll be your own lookout. But he's to wait till I come. If the ice does bear, it won't bear any too well; and I'm responsible for Wiggins. I promised Mr. Carrington to look after him," said the Terror in tones of stern gravity.

Erebus tossed her head and said in a somewhat rebellious tone: "As if I couldn't take care of him just as well as you. I'm as old as you."

"Perhaps," said the Terror doubtfully. "But you are a girl; there's no getting over it; and it does make a difference."

Erebus turned and scowled at him as he moved toward the door; and she scowled at the door after he had gone through it and shut it firmly behind him. She hated to be reminded that she was a girl. The reminder rankled at intervals during her lessons; and twice Mrs. Dangerfield asked her what was distressing her that she scowled so fiercely.

At noon her lessons came to an end; and in less than three minutes she was ready to go skating. She set out briskly across the common, and found Wiggins waiting for her at his father's garden-gate. He joined her in a fine enthusiasm for the ice and talked of the certainty of its bearing with the most hopeful confidence. She displayed an equal confidence; and they took their brisk way across the white meadows. More than usual Wiggins spurned the earth and advanced by leaps and bounds. His blue eyes were shining very brightly in the cold winter sunlight.

In ten minutes they came to Pringle's pond. The wind had swept the ice fairly clear of snow; and it looked smooth and very tempting. Also it looked quite thick and strong. Erebus stepped on to it gingerly, found that it bore her, and tested it with some care. She even jumped up and down on it. It cracked, but it did not break; and she told herself that ice always cracks, more or less. She set about putting on her skates; and the joyful Wiggins, all fear of disappointment allayed, followed her example.

When presently he stood upright in them ready to take the ice, she looked at him doubtfully, then tossed her head impatiently. No; she would not tell him that the Terror had charged her not to let him skate till he came. . . . She could look after him quite as well as the Terror. . . . She had tested the ice thoroughly. . . . It was perfectly safe.

Wiggins slid down the bank on to the ice; and she followed him. The ice cracked somewhat noisily at their weight, and at intervals it cracked again. Erebus paid no heed to its cracking beyond telling Wiggins not to go far from the edge. She skated round and across the pond several times, then settled down to make a figure of eight, resolved to have it scored deeply in the ice before the Terror came. Wiggins skated about the pond.

She had been at work some time and had got so far with her figure of eight that it was already distinctly marked, when there was a crash and a shrill cry from Wiggins. She turned sharply to see the water welling up out of a dark triangular hole on the other side of the pond, where a row of pollard willows had screened the ice from the full keenness of the wind.

Wiggins was in that hole under the water.

She screamed and dashed toward it. She had nearly reached it when his head came up above the surface; and he clutched at the ice. Two more steps and a loud crack gave her pause. It flashed on her that if she went near it, she would merely widen the hole and be helpless in the water herself.

"Hold on! Hold on!" she cried as she stopped ten yards from the hole; and then she sent a shrill piercing scream from all her lungs ringing through the still winter air.

She screamed again and yet again. Wiggins' face rose above the edge of the ice; and he gasped and spluttered. Then she sank down gently, at full length, face downward on the ice, and squirmed slowly, spread out so as to distribute her weight over as wide a surface as possible, toward the hole. Half a minute's cautious squirming brought her hands to the edge of it; and with a sob of relief she grasped his wrists. The ice bent under her weight, but it did not break. The icy water, welling out over it, began to drench her arms and chest.

Very gently she tried to draw Wiggins out over the ice; but she could not. She could get no grip on it with her toes to drag from.

Wiggins' little face, two feet from her own, was very white; and his teeth chattered.

She set her teeth and strove to find a hold for her slipping toes. She could not.

"C-c-can't you p-p-pull m-m-me out?" chattered Wiggins.

"No, not yet," she said hoarsely. "But it's all right. The Terror will be here in a minute."

She raised her head as high as she could and screamed again.

She listened with all her ears for an answer. A bird squeaked shrilly on the other side of the field; there was no other sound. Wiggins' white face was now bluish round the mouth; and his eyes were full of fear. Again she kicked about for a grip, in vain.

"It's d-d-dreadfully c-c-cold," said Wiggins in a very faint voice; he began to sob; and his eyes looked very dully into hers.

She knew that it was dreadfully cold; her drenched arms and chest were dreadfully cold; and he was in that icy water to his shoulders.

"Try to stick it out! Don't give in! It's only a minute or two longer! The Terror *must* come!" she cried fiercely.

His eyes gazed at her piteously; and she began to sob without feeling ashamed of it. Then his eyes filled with that dreadful look of hopeless bewildered distress of a very sick child; and they rolled in their sockets scanning the cold sky in desperate appeal.

They terrified Erebus beyond words. She screamed, and then she screamed and screamed. Wiggins' face was a mere white blur through her blinding tears of terror.

She knew nothing till her ankles were firmly gripped; and the Terror cried loudly: "Stop that row!"

She felt him tug at her ankles but not nearly strongly enough to stir her and Wiggins. He, too, could get no hold on the ice with his toes.

Then he cried: 'Squirm round to the left. I'll help you."

He made his meaning clearer by tugging her ankles toward the left; and she squirmed in that direction as fast as she dared over the bending ice.

In less than half a minute the Terror got his feet among the roots of a willow, gripped them with his toes, and with a strong and steady pull began to draw them toward the bank. The ice creaked as Wiggins' chest came over the edge of the hole; but it did not break; and his body once flat on the ice, the Terror hauled them to the side of the pond easily. He dragged Erebus, still by the ankles, half up the bank to get most of her weight off the ice. Then he stepped down on to it and picked up Wiggins. Erebus' stiff fingers still grasped his wrists; and they did not open easily to let them go.

The Terror took one look at the deathly faintly-breathing Wiggins; then he pulled off his woolen gloves, drew his knife from his pocket, opened the blade with his teeth for quickness' sake, tossed it to Erebus and cried: "Cut off his skates! Pull off his boots and stockings!"

Then with swift deft fingers he stripped off Wiggins' coat, jersey and waistcoat, pulled on his gloves, caught up a handful of snow and began to rub his chest violently. In the spring the Twins had attended a course of the St. John's Ambulance Society lectures, and among other things had learned how to treat those dying from exposure. The Terror was the quicker dealing with Wiggins since he had so often been the subject on which he and Erebus had practised many kinds of first-aid.

He rubbed hard till the skin reddened with the blood flowing back into it. Erebus with feeble fumbling fingers (she was almost spent with cold and terror) cut the straps of his skates and the laces of his boots, pulled them off, pulled off his stockings, and rubbed feebly at his legs. The Terror turned Wiggins over and rubbed his back violently till the blood reddened that. Wiggins uttered a little gasping grunt.

Forthwith the Terror pulled off his own coat and jersey and put them on Wiggins; then he pulled off Wiggins' knicker-bockers and rubbed his thighs till they reddened; then he pulled off his stockings and pulled them on Wiggins' legs. The stockings came well up his thighs; and the Terror's coat and jersey came well down them. Wiggins was completely covered. But the Terror was not satisfied; he called on Erebus for her stockings and pulled them on Wiggins over his own; then he took her jacket and tied it round Wiggins' waist by the sleeves.

Wiggins was much less blue; and the whiteness of his cheeks was no longer a dead waxen color. He opened his eyes twice and shut them feebly.

The Terror shook him, and shouted: "Come on, old chap! Make an effort! We want to get you home!"

With that he raised him on to his feet, put his own cap well over Wiggins' cold wet head, slipped an arm round him under his shoulder, bade Erebus support him in like manner on the other side; and they set off toward the village half carrying, half dragging him along. They went slowly for Wiggins' feet dragged feebly and almost helplessly along. Their arms round him helped warm him. It would have taken them a long time to haul him all the way to his home; but fortunately soon after they came out of Pringle's meadows on to the road, Jakes, the Great Deeping butcher, who supplies also Little Deeping and Muttle Deeping with meat, came clattering along in his cart. Wiggins was quickly hauled into it; and the three of them were at Mr. Carrington's in about four minutes.

As they hauled Wiggins along the garden path, the Terror, said to Erebus: "You bolt home as hard as you can go. You must be awfully wet and cold; and if you don't want to be laid up, the sooner you take some quinine and get to bed the better."

As soon therefore as she had helped Wiggins over the threshold she ran home as quickly as her legs, still stiff and cold, would carry her.

The arrival of the barelegged Terror in his waistcoat, bearing Wiggins as a half-animate bundle, set Mr. Carrington's house in an uproar. The Terror, as the expert in first-aid, took command of the cook and housemaid and Mr. Carrington himself. Wiggins was carried into the hot kitchen and rolled in a blanket with a hot water bottle at his feet. The cook was for two blankets and two hot water bottles; but the expert Terror insisted with a firmness there was no bending that heat must be restored slowly. As Wiggins warmed he gave him warm brandy and water with a teaspoon. In ten minutes Wiggins was quite animate, able to talk faintly, trying not to cry with the pain of returning circulation.

The Terror sent the cook and housemaid to get the sheets off his bed and warm the blankets. In another five minute's Mr. Carrington carried Wiggins up to it, and gave him a dose of ammoniated quinine. Presently he fell asleep.

The Terror had taken his coat off Wiggins; but he was still without stockings and a jersey. He borrowed stockings and a sweater from Mr. Carrington, and now that the business of seeing after Wiggins was over, he told him how he had come to the pond to find Wiggins in the water and Erebus spread out on the ice, holding him back from sinking. He was careful not to tell him that he had forbidden Erebus to let Wiggins go on the ice; and when Mr. Carrington began to thank him for saving him, he insisted on giving all the credit to Erebus.

Mr. Carrington made him also take a dose of ammoniated quinine, and then further fortified him with cake and very agreeable port wine. On his way home the Terror went briskly round by Pringle's pond and picked up the skates and garments that had been left there. When he reached home he found that Erebus was in bed. She seemed little the worse for lying with her arms and chest in that icy water, keeping Wiggins afloat; and when she learned that Wiggins also seemed none the worse and was sleeping peacefully, she ate her lunch with a fair appetite.

The Terror did not point out that all the trouble had sprung from her disregard for his instructions; he only said: "I just told Mr. Carrington that Wiggins was already in the water when I got to the pond."

"That was awfully decent of you," said Erebus after a pause in which she had gathered the full bearing of his reticence.

CHAPTER VIII

AND THE MUTTLE DEEPING PEACHES

The dreadful fright she had suffered did not throw a cloud over the spirit of Erebus for as long as might have been expected. She was as quick as any one to realize that all's well that ends well; and Wiggins escaped lightly, with a couple of days in bed. The adventure, however, induced a change in her attitude to him; she was far less condescending with him than she had been; indeed she seemed to have acquired something of a proprietary interest in him and was uncommonly solicitous for his welfare. To such a point did this solicitude go that more than once he remonstrated bitterly with her for fussing about him.

During the rest of the winter, the spring and the early summer, their lives followed an even tenor: they did their lessons; they played their games; then tended the inmates of the cats' home, selling them as they grew big, and replacing the sold with threepenny kittens just able to lap.

In the spring they fished the free water of the Whittle, the little trout-stream that runs through the estate of the Morgans of Muttle Deeping Grange. The free water runs for rather more than half a mile on the Little Deeping side of Muttle Deeping; and the Twins fished it with an assiduity and a skill which set the villagers grumbling that they left no fish for any one else. Also the Twins tried to get leave to fish Sir James Morgan's preserved water, higher up the stream. But Mr. Hilton, the agent of the estate, was very firm in his refusal to give them leave: for no reason that the Twins could see, since Sir James was absent, shooting big game in Africa. They resented the refusal bitterly; it seemed to them a wanton waste of the stream. It was some consolation to them to make a well-judged raid one early morning on the strawberry-beds in one of the walled gardens of Muttle Deeping Grange.

About the middle of June the Terror went to London on a visit to their Aunt Amelia. Sir Maurice Falconer and Miss Hendersyde saw to it that it was not the unbroken series of visits to cats' homes Lady Ryehampton had arranged for him; and he enjoyed it very much. On his return he was able to assure the interested Erebus that their aunt's parrot still said "dam" with a perfectly accurate, but monotonous iteration.

Soon after his return the news was spread abroad that Sir James Morgan had let Muttle Deeping Grange. In the life of the Deeping villages the mere letting of Muttle Deeping Grange was no unimportant event, but the inhabitants of Great Deeping, Muttle Deeping (possibly a corruption of Middle Deeping), and Little Deeping were stirred to the very depths of their being when the news came that it had been let to a German princess. The women, at any rate, awaited her coming with the liveliest interest and curiosity, emotions dashed some way from their fine height when they learned that Princess Elizabeth, of Cassel-Nassau, was only twelve years and seven months old.

The Twins did not share the excited curiosity of their neighbors. Resenting deeply the fact that the tenant of Muttle Deeping was a *German* princess, they assumed an attitude of cold aloofness in the matter, and refused to be interested or impressed. Erebus was more resentful than the Terror; and it is to be suspected that the high patriotic spirit she displayed in the matter was in some degree owing to the fact that Mrs. Blenkinsop, who came one afternoon to tea, gushing information about the grandfathers, grandmothers, parents, uncles, cousins and aunts of the princess, ended by saying, with meaning, "And what a model she will be to the little girls of the neighborhood!"

Erebus told the Terror that things were indeed come to a pretty pass when it was suggested to an English girl, a Dangerfield, too, that she should model herself on a German.

"I don't suppose it would really make any difference who you modeled yourself on," said the Terror, desirous rather of being frank than grammatical.

When presently the princess came to the Grange, the lively curiosity of her neighbors was gratified by but imperfect visions of her. She did not, as they had expected, attend any of the three churches, for she had brought with her her own Lutheran pastor. They only saw her on her afternoon drives, a stiff little figure, thickly veiled against the sun, sitting bolt upright in the victoria beside the crimson baroness (crimson in face; she wore black) in whose charge she had come to England.

They learned presently that the princess had come to Muttle Deeping for her health; that she was delicate and her doctors feared lest she should develop consumption; they hoped that a few weeks in the excellent Deeping air would strengthen her. The news abated a little the cold hostility of Erebus; but the Twins paid but little attention to their young neighbor.

Their mother was finding the summer trying; she was

sleeping badly, and her appetite was poor. Doctor Arbuthnot put her on a light diet; and in particular he ordered her to eat plenty of fruit. It was not the best season for fruit: strawberries were over and raspberries were coming to an end. Mrs. Dangerfield made shift to do with bananas. The Twins were annoyed that this was the best that could be done to carry out the doctor's orders; but there seemed no help for it.

It was in the afternoon, a sweltering afternoon, after the doctor's visit that, as the Twins, bent on an aimless ride, were lazily wheeling their bicycles out of the cats' home, a sudden gleam came into the eyes of the Terror; and he said:

"I've got an idea!"

An answering light gleamed in the eyes of Erebus; and she cried joyfully; "Thank goodness! I was beginning to get afraid that nothing was ever going to occur to us again. I thought it was the hot weather. What is it?"

"Those Germans," said the Terror darkly. "Now that they've got the Grange, why shouldn't we make a raid on the peach-garden. They say the Grange peaches are better than any hothouse ones; and Watkins told me they ripen uncommon early. They're probably ripe now."

"That's a splendid idea! It will just teach those Germans!" cried Erebus; and her piquant face was bright with the sterling spirit of the patriot. Then after a pause she added reluctantly: "But if the princess is an invalid, perhaps she ought to have all the peaches herself."

"She couldn't want all of them. Why we couldn't. There are hundreds," said the Terror quickly. "And they're the very thing for Mum. Bananas are all very well in their way; but they're not like real fruit."

"Of course; Mum *must* have them," said Erebus with decision. "But how are we going to get into the peach-garden? The door in the wall only opens on the inside."

"We're not. I've worked it out. Now you just hurry up and get some big leaves to put the peaches in. Mum will like them ever so much better with the bloom on, though it doesn't really make any difference to the taste."

Erebus ran into the kitchen-garden and gathered big soft leaves of different kinds. When she came back she found the Terror tying the landing-net they had borrowed from the vicar for their trout-fishing, to the backbone of his bicycle. She put the leaves into her bicycle basket, and they rode briskly to Muttle Deeping.

The Twins knew all the approaches to Muttle Deeping Grange well since they had spent several days in careful scouting before they had made their raid earlier in the summer on its strawberry beds. A screen of trees runs down from the home wood along the walls of the gardens; and the Twins, after coming from the road in the shelter of the home wood, came down the wall behind that screen of trees.

About the middle of the peach-garden the Terror climbed on to a low bough, raised his head with slow caution above the wall, and surveyed the garden. It was empty and silent, save for a curious snoring sound that disquieted him little, since he ascribed it to some distant pig.

He stepped on to a higher branch, leaned over the wall, and surveyed the golden burden of the tree beneath him. The ready Erebus handed the landing-net up to him. He chose his peach, the ripest he could see; slipped the net under it, flicked it, lifted the peach in it over the wall, and lowered it down to Erebus, who made haste to roll it in a leaf and lay it gently in her bicycle basket. The Terror netted another and another and another.

The garden was not as empty as he believed. On a garden chair in the little lawn in the middle of it sat the Princess Elizabeth hidden from him by the thick wall of a pear tree, and in a chair beside her, sat, or rather sprawled, her guardian, the Baroness Frederica Von Aschersleben, who was following faithfully the doctor's instructions that her little charge should spend her time in the open air, but was doing her best to bring it about that the practise should do her as little good as possible by choosing the sultriest and most airless spot on the estate because it was so admirably adapted to her own comfortable sleeping.

The baroness added nothing to the old-world charm of the garden. Her eyes were shut, her mouth was open, her face was most painfully crimson, and from her short, but extremely tip-tilted nose, came the sound of snoring which the Terror had ascribed to some distant pig.

The princess was warmly—very warmly—dressed for the sweltering afternoon and sweltering spot; little beads of sweat stood on her brow; the story-book she had been trying to read lay face downward in her lap; and she was looking round the simmering garden with a look of intolerable discomfort and boredom on her pretty pale face.

Then a moving object came into the range of her vision, just beyond the end-of the wall of pear tree—a moving object against the garden wall. She could not see clearly what it was; but it seemed to her that a peach rose and vanished over the top of the wall. She stared at the part of the wall whence it had risen; and in a few seconds another peach seemed to rise and disappear.

This curious behavior of English peaches so roused her curiosity that, in spite of the heat, she rose and walked quietly to the end of the wall of pear-tree. As she came beyond it, she saw, leaning over the wall, a fair-haired boy. Even as she saw him something rose and vanished over the wall far too swiftly for her to see that it was a landing-net.

Surprise did not rob the Terror of his politeness; he smiled amicably, raised his cap and said in his most agreeable tone: "How do you do?"

He did not know how much the princess had seen, and he was not going to make admission of guilt by a hasty and perhaps needless flight, provoke pursuit and risk his peaches.

"How do you do?" said the princess a little haughtily, hesitating. "What are you doing up there?"

"I'm looking at the garden," said the Terror truthfully, but not quite accurately; for he was looking much more at the princess.

She gazed at him; her brow knitted in a little perplexed frown. She thought that he had been taking the peaches; but she was not sure; and his serene guileless face and limpid blue eyes gave the suspicion the lie. She thought that he looked a nice boy.

He gazed at her with growing interest and approval—as much approval as one could give to a girl. The Princess Elizabeth had beautiful gray eyes; and though her pale cheeks were a little hollow, and the line from the cheek-bone to the corner of the chin was so straight that it made her face almost triangular, it was a pretty face. She looked fragile; and he felt sorry for her.

"This garden's very hot," he said. "It's like holding one's face over an oven."

"Oh, it is," said the princess, with impatient weariness.

"Yet there's quite a decent little breeze blowing over the top of the walls," said the Terror.

The princess sighed, and they gazed at each other with curious examining eyes. Certainly he looked a nice boy.

"I tell you what: come out into the wood. I know an awfully cool place. You'd find it very refreshing," said the Terror in the tone of one who has of a sudden been happily inspired.

The princess looked back along the wall of pear tree irresolutely at the sleeping baroness. The sight of that richly crimson face made the garden feel hotter than ever.

"Do come. My sister's here, and it will be very jolly in the wood—the three of us," said the Terror in his most persuasive tone.

The princess hesitated, and again she looked back at the sleeping but unbeautiful baroness; then she said with a truly German frankness:

"Are you well-born?"

The Terror smiled a little haughtily in his turn and said slowly: "Well, from what Mrs. Blenkinsop said, the Dangerfields were barons in the Weald before they were any Hohenzollerns. And they did very well at Crecy and Agincourt, too," he added pensively.

The princess seemed reassured; but she still hesitated.

"Suppose the baroness were to wake?" she said.

A light of understanding brightened the Terror's face: "Oh, is that the baroness snoring? I thought it was a pig," he said frankly. "She won't wake for another hour. Nobody snoring like that could."

The assurance seemed to disperse the last doubts of the princess. She cast one more look back at her crimson Argus, and said: "Very goot; I will coom."

She walked to the door lower down the garden wall. When she came through it, she found the Twins wheeling their bicycles toward it. The Terror, in a very dignified fashion, introduced Erebus to her as Violet Anastasia Dangerfield, and himself as Hyacinth Wolfram Dangerfield. He gave their full and so little-used names because he felt that, in the case of a princess, etiquette demanded it. Then they moved along the screen of trees, up the side of the garden wall toward the wood.

The Twins shortened their strides to suit the pace of the princess, which was uncommonly slow. She kept looking from one to the other with curious, rather timid, pleased eyes. She saw the landing-net that Erebus had fastened to the backbone of the Terror's bicycle; but she saw no connection between it and the vanishing peaches.

They passed straight from the screen of trees through a gap into the home wood, a gap of a size to let them carry their bicycles through without difficulty, took a narrow, little used path into the depths of the wood, and moved down it in single file.

"I expect you never found this path," said the Terror to the princess who was following closely on the back wheel of his bicycle.

"No, I haf not found it. I haf never been in this wood till now," said the princess.

"You haven't been in this wood! But it's the home wood—the jolliest part of the estate," cried the Terror in the liveliest surprise. "And there are two paths straight into it from the gardens."

"But I stay always in the gardens," said the princess sedately. "The Baroness Von Aschersleben does not walk mooch; and she will not that I go out of sight of her."

"But you must get awfully slack, sticking in the gardens all the time," said Erebus.

"Slack? What is slack?" said the princess.

"She means feeble," said the Terror. "But all the same those gardens are big enough; there's plenty of room to run about in them."

"But I do not run. It is not dignified. The Baroness Von Aschersleben would be shocked," said the princess with a somewhat prim air.

"No wonder you're delicate," said Erebus, politely trying to keep a touch of contempt out of her tone, and failing.

"One can not help being delicate," said the princess.

"I don't know," said the Terror doubtfully. "If you're in the open air a lot and do run about, you don't *keep* delicate. Wiggins used to be delicate, but he isn't now."

"Who is Wiggins?" said the princess.

"He's a friend of ours—not so old as we are—quite a little boy," said Erebus in a patronizing tone which Wiggins, had he been present, would have resented with extreme bitterness. "Besides, Doctor Arbuthnot told Mrs. Blenkinsop that if you were always in the open air, playing with children of your own age, you'd soon get strong."

"That's what I've come to England for," said the princess.

"I don't think there's much chance of your getting strong in that peach-garden. It didn't feel to me like the open air at all," said the Terror firmly.

"But it is the open air," said the princess.

They came out of the narrow path they had been following into a broader one, and presently they turned aside from that at the foot of a steep and pathless bank. The Twins started up it as if it were neither here nor there to them; as, indeed, it was not.

But the princess stopped short, and said in a tone of dismay:

"Am I to climb this?"

The Terror stopped, looked at her dismayed face, set his bicycle against the trunk of a tree, and said:

"I'll help you up."

With that, dismissing etiquette from his mind, he slipped his arm round the slender waist of the princess, and firmly hauled her to the top of the bank. He relieved her of most of the effort needed to mount it; but none the less she reached the top panting a little.

"You certainly aren't in very good training," he said rather sadly.

"Training? What is training?" said the princess.

"It's being fit," said Erebus in a faintly superior tone.

"And what is being fit?" said the princess.

"It's being strong—and well—and able to run miles and miles," said Erebus raising her voice to make her meaning clearer.

"You needn't shout at her," said the Terror.

"I'm trying to make her understand," said Erebus firmly.

"But I do understand—when it is not the slang you are using. I know English quite well," said the princess.

"You certainly speak it awfully well," said the Terror politely.

He went down the bank and hauled up his bicycle. They went a little deeper into the wood and reached their goal, the banks of a small pool.

They sat down in a row, and the princess looked at its cool water, in the cool green shade of the tall trees, with refreshed eyes.

"This *is* different," she said with a faint little sigh of pleasure.

"Yes; this is the real open air," said the Terror.

"But I do get lots of open air," protested the princess. "Why, I sleep with my window open—at least that much." She held out her two forefingers some six inches apart. "The baroness did not like it. She said it was very dangerous and would give me the chills. But Doctor Arbuthnot said that it must be open. I think I sleep better."

"We have our bedroom windows as wide open as they'll go; and then they're not wide enough in this hot weather," said Erebus in the tone of superiority that was beginning to sound galling.

"I think if you took off your hat and jacket, you'd be cooler still," said the Terror rather quickly.

The princess hesitated a moment; then obediently she took off her hat and jacket, and breathed another soft sigh of pleasure. She had quite lost her air of discomfort and boredom. Her eyes were shining brightly; and her pale cheeks were a little flushed with the excitement of her situation.

It is by no means improbable that the Twins, as well-brought-up children, were aware that it is not etiquette to speak to royal personages unless they first speak to you. If they were, they did not let that knowledge stand in the way of the gratification of their healthy curiosity. It may be they felt that in the free green wood the etiquette of courts was out of place. At any rate they did not let it trammel them; and since their healthy curiosity was of the liveliest kind they submitted the princess to searching, even exhaustive, interrogation about the life of a royal child at a German court.

They questioned her about the hour she rose, the breakfast

Edgar Jepson

she ate, the lessons she learned, the walks she took, the lunch she ate, the games she played, her afternoon occupations, her dolls, her pets, her tea, her occupations after tea, her dinner, her occupations after dinner, the hour she went to bed.

There seemed nothing impertinent in their curiosity to the princess; it was only natural that every detail of the life of a person of her importance should be of the greatest interest to less fortunate mortals. She was not even annoyed by their carelessness of etiquette in not waiting to be spoken to before they asked a question. Indeed she enjoyed answering their questions very much, for it was seldom that any one displayed such a genuine interest in her; it was seldom, indeed, that she found herself on intimate human terms with any of her fellow creatures. She had neither brothers nor sisters; and she had never had any really sympathetic playmates. The children of Cassel-Nassau were always awed and stiff in her society; their minds were harassed by the fear lest they should be guilty of some appalling breach of etiquette. The manner of the Twins, therefore, was a pleasant change for her. They were polite, but quite unconstrained; and the obsequious people by whom she had always been surrounded had never displayed that engaging quality, save when, like the baroness, they were safely asleep in her presence.

But her account of her glories did not have the effect on her new friends she looked for. As she exposed more and more of the trammeling net of etiquette in which from her rising to her going to bed she was enmeshed, their faces did not fill with the envy she would have found so natural on them; they grew gloomy.

At the end of the interrogation Erebus heaved a great sigh, and said with heart-felt conviction:

"Well, thank goodness, I'm not a princess! It must be perfectly awful!"

"It must be nearly as bad to be a prince," said the Terror in the gloomy tone of one who has lost a dear illusion.

The princess could not believe her ears; she stared at the Twins with parted lips and amazed incredulous eyes. Their words had given her the shock of her short lifetime. As far as memory carried her back, she had been assured, frequently and solemnly, that to be a princess, a German princess, a Hohenzollern princess, was the most glorious and delightful lot a female human being could enjoy, only a little less glorious and delightful than the lot of a German prince.

"B-b-but it's sp-p-plendid to be a princess! Everybody says so!" she stammered.

"They were humbugging you. You've just made it quite clear that it's horrid in every kind of way. Why, you can't do any single thing you want to. There's always somebody messing about you to see that you don't," said Erebus with cold decision.

"B-b-but one is a *p-p-princess*," stammered the princess, with something of the wild look of one beneath whose feet the firm earth has suddenly given way.

The Terror perceived her distress; and he set about soothing it.

"You're forgetting the food," he said quickly to Erebus. "I don't suppose she ever has to eat cold mutton; and I expect she can have all the sweets and ices she wants."

"Of course," said the princess; and then she went on quickly:

"B-b-but it isn't what you have to eat that makes it so—so—so important being a princess. It's—"

"But it's awfully important what you have to eat!" cried the Terror.

"I should jolly well think so!" cried Erebus.

The princess tried hard to get back to the moral sublimities of her exalted station; but the Twins would not have it. They kept her firmly to the broad human questions of German cookery and sweets. The princess, used to having information poured into her by many elderly but bespectacled gentlemen and ladies, was presently again enjoying her new part of dispenser of information. Her cheeks were faintly flushed; and her eyes were sparkling in an animated face.

In these interrogations and discussions the time had slipped away unheeded by the interested trio. The crimson baroness had awakened, missed her little charge, and waddled off into the house in search of her. A slow search of the house and gardens revealed the fact that she was not in them. As soon as this was clear the baroness fell into a panic and insisted that the whole household should sally forth in search of her.

The princess was earnestly engaged in an effort to make quite dear to the Twins the exact nature of one of the obscure kinds of German tartlet, a kind, indeed, only found in the principality of Cassel-Nassau, where the keen ears of the Terror caught the sound of a distant voice calling out.

He rose sharply to his feet and said: "Listen! There's some one calling. I expect they've missed you and you'll have to be getting back."

The princess rose reluctantly. Then her face clouded; and she said in a tone of faint dismay: "Oh, dear! How annoyed the baroness will be!"

"You take a great deal too much notice of that baroness," said Erebus.

"But I have to; she's my—my *gouvernante*," said the princess.

"I don't see what good it is being a princess, if you do just what baronesses tell you all the time," said Erebus coldly.

The princess looked at her rather helplessly; she had never thought of rebelling.

"I don't think I should tell her that you've been with us. She mightn't think we were good for you. Some people round here don't seem to understand us," said the Terror suavely.

The princess looked from one to the other, hesitating with puckered brow; and then, with a touch of appeal in her tone, she said, "Are you coming to-morrow?"

The Twins looked at each other doubtfully. They had no plans for the morrow; but they had hopes that Fortune would find them some more exciting occupation than discussing Germany with one of its inhabitants.

At their hesitation the princess' face fell woefully; and the appeal in it touched the Terror's heart.

"We should like to come very much," he said.

The face of the princess brightened; and her grateful eyes shone on him.

"I don't think I shall be able to come," said Erebus with the important air of one burdened with many affairs.

The face of the princess did not fall again; she said: "But if your brother comes?"

"Oh, I'll come, anyhow," said the Terror.

The voice called again from the wood below, louder.

"Oh, it isn't the baroness. It's Miss Lambart," said the princess in a tone of relief.

"You take too much notice of that baroness," said Erebus again firmly. "Who is Miss Lambart?"

"She's my English lady-in-waiting. I always have one when I'm in England, of course. I like her. She tries to amuse me. But the baroness doesn't like her," said the princess, and she sighed.

"Come along, I'll help you down the bank and take you pretty close to Miss Lambart. It wouldn't do for her to know of this place. It's our secret lair," said the Terror.

"I see," said the princess.

They walked briskly to the edge of the steep bank; and he half carried her down it; and he led her through the wood toward the drive from which Miss Lambart had called. As they went he adjured her to confine herself to the simple if incomplete statement that she had been walking in the wood. His last words to her, as they stood on the edge of the drive, were:

"Don't you stand so much nonsense from that baroness."

Miss Lambart called again; the princess stepped into the drive and found her thirty yards away. The Terror slipped noiselessly away through the undergrowth.

Miss Lambart turned at the sound of the princess' footsteps, and said: "Oh, here you are, Highness. We've all been hunting for you. The baroness thought you were lost."

"I thought I would walk in the wood," said the princess demurely.

"It certainly seems to have done you good. You're looking brighter and fresher than you've looked since you've been down here."

"The wood is real open air," said the princess.

Edgar Jepson

CHAPTER IX

AND THE CAUSE OF FREEDOM

The Terror returned to Erebus and found her stretched at her ease, eating a peach.

"I should have liked one a good deal sooner," he said, as he took one from the basket. "But I didn't like to say anything about them. She mightn't have understood."

"It wouldn't have mattered if she hadn't," said Erebus somewhat truculently.

She was feeling some slight resentment that their new acquaintance had so plainly preferred the Terror to her.

"She's not a bad kid," said the Terror thoughtfully.

"She's awfully feeble. Why, you had to carry her up this bit of a bank. She's not any use to us," said Erebus in a tone of contempt. "In fact, if we were to have much to do with her, I expect we should find her a perfect nuisance."

"Perhaps. Still we may as well amuse her a bit. She seems to be having a rotten time with that old red baroness and all that etiquette," said the Terror in a kindly tone.

"She needn't stand it, if she doesn't like it. I shouldn't," said Erebus coldly; then her face brightened, and she added: "I tell you what though: it would be rather fun to teach her to jump on that old red baroness."

"Yes," said the Terror doubtfully. "But I expect she'd take a lot of teaching. I don't think she's the kind of kid to do much jumping on people."

"Oh, you never know. We can always try," said Erebus cheerfully.

"Yes," said the Terror.

Warmed by this noble resolve, they moved quietly out of the wood. It was not so difficult a matter as it may sound to move, even encumbered by bicycles, about the home wood, for it was not so carefully preserved as the woods farther away from the Grange; indeed, the keepers paid but little attention to it. The Twins moved out of it safely and returned home with easy minds: it did not occur to either of them that they had been treating a princess with singular firmness. Nor were they at all troubled about the acquisition of the peaches since some curious mental kink prevented them from perceiving that the law of meum and tuum applied to fruit.

Mrs. Dangerfield was presented with only two peaches at tea that afternoon; and she took it that the Twins had ridden into Rowington and bought them for her there. When two more were forthcoming for her dessert after dinner, she reproached them gently for spending so much of their salary for "overseeing" on her. The Twins said nothing. It was only when two more peaches came up on her breakfast tray that she began to suspect that they had come by the ways of warfare and not of trade. Then, having already eaten four of them, it was a little late to inquire and protest. Moreover, if there had been a crime, the Twins had admitted her to a full share in it by letting her eat the fruit of it. Plainly it was once more an occasion for saying nothing.

On the next afternoon Erebus set out with the Terror to Muttle Deeping home wood early enough; but owing to the matter of a young rabbit who met them on their way, they kept the princess waiting twenty minutes. This was, indeed, a new experience to her; but she did not complain to them of this unheard-of breach of etiquette. She was doubtful how the complaint would be received at any rate by Erebus.

They betook themselves at once to the cool and shady pool; and since the sensation was no longer new and startling, the princess found it rather pleasant to be hauled up the bank by the Terror. There was something very satisfactory in his strength. Again they settled themselves comfortably on the bank of the pool.

They were in the strongest contrast to one another. Beside the clear golden tan of the Terror and the deeper gipsy-like brown of Erebus the pale face of the princess looked waxen. The blue linen blouse, short serge skirt and bare head and legs of Erebus and the blue linen shirt, serge knickerbockers and bare head and legs of the Terror gave them an air not only of coolness but also of a workmanlike freedom of limb. In her woolen blouse, brown serge jacket and skirt, woolen stockings and heavily-trimmed drooping hat the poor little princess looked a swaddled sweltering doll melting in the heat.

She needed no pressing to take off her jacket and hat; and was pleased by the Terror's observing that it was just silly to wear a hat at all when one had such thick hair as she. But she was some time acting on Erebus' suggestion that she should also pull off her stockings and be more comfortable still.

At last she pulled them off, and for once comfortable, she began to tell of the fuss the excited baroness had made the day before about her having gone alone into such a fearful and dangerous place as the home wood.

"I tell you what: you've spoilt that baroness," said the Terror when she came to the end of her tale; and he spoke with firm conviction.

"But she's my *gouvernante*. I have to do as she bids," protested the princess.

"That's all rubbish. You're the princess; and other people ought to do what you tell them; and no old baroness should make you do any silly thing you don't want to. She wouldn't me," said Erebus with even greater conviction than the Terror had shown.

"I don't think she would," said the princess with a faint sigh; and she looked at Erebus with envious eyes. "But when she starts making a fuss and gets so red and excited, she—she— rather frightens me."

"It would take a lot more than that to frighten me," said Erebus with a very cold ferocity.

"I rather like people like that. I think they look so funny when they're really red and excited," said the Terror gently. "But what you've got to do is to stand up to her."

"Stand up to her?" said the princess, puzzled by the idiom.

"Tell her that you don't care what she says," said the Terror.

"Cheek her," said Erebus.

"I couldn't. It would be too difficult," said the princess, shaking her head.

"Of course it isn't easy at first; but you'll be surprised to find how soon you'll get used to shutting her up," said the Terror. "But I don't believe in cheeking her unless she gets very noisy. I believe in being quite polite but not giving way."

"She is very noisy," said the princess.

"Oh, then you'll have to shout at her. It's the only way. But mind you only have rows when you're in the right about something," said the Terror. "Then she'll soon learn to leave you alone. It's no good having a row when you're in the wrong."

"I think it's best always to have a row," said Erebus with an air of wide experience.

"Well, it isn't—at least it wouldn't be for the princess—she's not like you," said the Terror quickly.

"Oh, no: not always—only when one is in the right. I see that," said the princess. "But what should I have a row about?"

The Twins puckered their brows as they cudgeled their brains for a pretext for an honest row.

Presently the Terror said: "Why don't you make them let you have some one to play with? It's silly being as dull as you are. What's the good of being a princess, if you haven't any friends?"

"Oh, yes!" cried the princess; and her cheeks flushed, and her eyes sparkled. "It would be nice! You and Erebus could come to tea with me and sooper and loonch often and again!"

The Twins looked at each other with eyes full of a sudden dismay. It was not in their scheme of things as they should be that they should go to the Grange in the immaculate morning dress of an English boy and girl, and spend stiff hours in the presence of a crimson baroness.

"That wouldn't do at all," said the Terror quickly. "You had better not tell them anything at all about us. They wouldn't let us come to the Grange; and they'd stop you coming here. It's ever so much nicer meeting secretly like this."

"But it would be very nice to meet at the Grange as well as here," said the princess, who felt strongly that she could not have enough of this good thing.

"It couldn't be done. They wouldn't have us at the Grange," said Erebus, supporting the Terror.

"But why not?" said the princess in surprise.

"The people about here don't understand us," said the Terror somewhat sadly. "They'd think we should be bad for you."

"But it is not so! You are ever so good to me!" cried the princess hotly.

"It's no good. You couldn't make grown-ups see that—you know what they are. No; you'd much better leave it alone, and sit tight and meet us here," said the Terror.

The princess sat thoughtful and frowning for a little while; then she sighed and said: "Well, I will do what you say. You know more about it."

"That's all right," said the Terror, greatly relieved.

There was a short silence; then he said thoughtfully: "I tell you what: it would be a good thing if you were to get some muscle on you. Suppose we taught you some exercises. You could practise them at home; and soon you'd be able to do things when you were with us."

"What things?" said the princess.

"Oh, you'd be able to run—and jump. Why we might even be able to teach you to climb," said the Terror with a touch of enthusiasm in his tone as the loftier heights of philanthropy loomed upon his inner vision.

"Oh, that would be nice!" cried the princess. Forthwith the Twins set about teaching her some of the exercises which go to the making of muscle; and the princess was a painstaking pupil. In spite of the seeds of revolt they had sown in her heart, she was eager to get back to the peach-garden before the baroness should awake, or at any rate before she should have satisfied herself that her charge was not in the house or about the gardens. The Terror therefore conducted her down the screen of trees to the door in the wall. She had left it unlatched; and he pushed it open gently. There was no sound of snoring: the baroness had awoke and left the garden.

"I expect she is still looking for me in the house," said the princess calmly. "They'd be shouting if she weren't."

"Yes. I say; do you want *all* these peaches?" said the Terror, looking round the loaded walls.

"Me? No. I have a peach for breakfast and another for lunch. But I don't care for peaches much. It's the way the baroness eats them, I think—the juice roonning down, you know. And she eats six or seven always."

"That woman's a pig. I thought she looked like one," said the Terror with conviction. "But if you don't want them all, may I have some for my mother? The doctor has ordered her fruit; and she's very fond of peaches."

"Oh, yes; take some for your mother and yourself and Erebus. Take them all," said the princess with quick generosity.

"Thank you; but a dozen will be heaps," said the Terror.

The princess helped him gather them and lay them in a large cabbage-leaf; and then they bade each other good-by at the garden-gate.

The Twins returned home in triumph with the golden spoil. But when she was provided with two peaches for seven meals in succession, Mrs. Dangerfield could no longer eat them with a mind at ease, and she asked the Twins how they came by them. They assured her that they had been given to them by a friend but that the name of the donor must remain a secret. She knew that they would not lie to her; and thinking it likely that they came from either the squire or the vicar, both of whom took an uncommonly lively interest in her, judging from the fact that either of them had asked her to marry him more than once, she went on eating the peaches with a clear conscience.

The next afternoon the Twins devoted themselves to strengthening the princess' spirit with no less ardor than they devoted themselves to strengthening her body. They adjured her again and again to thrust off the yoke of the baroness. The last pregnant words of Erebus to her were: "You just call her an old red pig, and see."

Their efforts in the cause of freedom bore fruit no later than that very evening. The princess was dining with the Baroness Von Aschersleben and Miss Lambart; and the baroness, who was exceedingly jealous of Miss Lambart, had interrupted her several times in her talk with the princess; and she had done it rudely. The princess, who wanted to hear Miss Lambart talk, was annoyed. They had reached dessert; and Miss Lambart was congratulating her on the improvement in her appetite since she had just made an excellent meal, and said that it must be the air of Muttle Deeping. The baroness uttered a loud and contemptuous snort, and filled her plate with peaches. The princess looked at her with an expression of great dislike. The baroness gobbled up one peach with a rapidity almost inconceivable in a human being, and very noisily, and was midway through the second when the princess spoke.

"I want some children to play with," she said.

Briskly and with the sound of a loud unpleasant sob the baroness gulped down the other half of the peach, and briskly she said: "Zere are no children in zis country, your Royal Highness."

It was the custom for the princess to speak and hear only English in England.

"But I see plenty of children when I drive," said the princess.

"Zey are nod children; zey are nod 'igh an' well-born," said the baroness in rasping tones.

"Then you must find some high and well-born children for me to play with," said the princess.

"Moost? Moost?" cried the baroness in a high voice. "Bud

eed ees whad I know ees goot for you."

"They're good for me," said the princess firmly. "And you must find them."

The baroness was taken aback by this so sudden and unexpected display of firmness in her little charge; her face darkened to a yet richer crimson; and she cried in a loud blustering voice: "Bud eed ees eembossible whad your royal highness ask! Zere are no 'igh an' well-born children 'ere. Zey are een Loondon."

"Well, you must send for some," said the princess, who, having taken the first step, was finding it pleasant to be firm.

"Moost? Moost? I do nod know whad ees 'appen to you, your Royal Highness. I say eed ees eembossible!" shouted the baroness; and she banged on the table with her fist.

"But surely her highness' request is a very natural one, Baroness; and there must be some nice children in the neighborhood if we were to look for them. Besides, Doctor Arbuthnot said that she ought to have children of her own age to play with," said Miss Lambart who had been pitying the lonely child and seized eagerly on this chance of helping her to the companionship she needed.

"Do nod indervere, Englanderin!" bellowed the baroness; and her crimson was enriched with streaks of purple. "I am in ze charge of 'er royal highness; and I zay zat she does not wiz zese children blay."

The fine gray eyes of the princess were burning with a somber glow. She was angry, and her mind was teeming with the instructions of her young mentors, especially with the more violent instructions of Erebus.

She gazed straight into the sparkling but blood-shot eyes of the raging baroness, and said in a somewhat uncertain voice but clearly enough:

"Old—red—peeg."

Miss Lambart started in her chair; the baroness uttered a gasping grunt; she blinked; she could not believe her ears.

"But whad—but whad—" she said faintly.

"Old—red—peeg," said the princess, somewhat pleased with the effect of the words, and desirous of deepening it.

"Bud whad ees eed zat 'appen?" muttered the bewildered baroness.

"If you do not find me children quickly, I shall write to my father that you do not as the English doctor bids; and you were ordered to do everything what the English doctor bids," said the princess in a sinister tone. "Then you will go back to Cassel-Nassau and the Baroness Hochfelden will be my *gouvernante*."

The baroness ground her teeth, but she trembled; it might easily happen, if the letter of the princess found the grand duke of Cassel-Nassau in the wrong mood, that she would lose this comfortable well-paid post, and the hated Baroness Hochfelden take it.

"Bud zere are no 'igh an' well-born children, your Royal Highness," she said in a far gentler, apologetic voice.

The princess frowned at her and said: "Mees Lambart will find them. Is it not, Mees Lambart?"

"I shall be charmed to try, Highness," said Miss Lambart readily.

"Do nod indervere! I veel zose childen vind myzelf!" snapped the baroness.

The princess rose, still quivering a little from the conflict, but glowing with the joy of victory. At the door she paused to say:

"And I want them soon—at once."

Then, though the baroness had many times forbidden her to tempt the night air, she went firmly out into the garden. The next morning at breakfast she again demanded children to play with.

Accordingly when Doctor Arbuthnot paid his visit that morning, the baroness asked him what children in the neighborhood could be invited to come to play with the princess. She only stipulated that they should be high and well-born.

"Well, of course the proper children to play with her would be the Twins—Mrs. Dangerfield's boy and girl. They're high and well-born enough. But I doubt that they could be induced to play with a little girl. They're independent young people. Besides, I'm not at all sure that they would be quite the playmates for a quiet princess. It would hardly do to expose an impressionable child like the princess to such— er—er ardent spirits. You might have her developing a spirit of freedom; and you wouldn't like that."

"*Mein Gott*, no!" said the baroness with warm conviction.

"Then there's Wiggins—Rupert Carrington. He's younger

and quieter but active enough. He'd soon teach her to run about."

"But is he well-born?" said the careful baroness.

"Well-born? He's a *Carrington*," said Doctor Arbuthnot with an impressive air that concealed well his utter ignorance of the ancestry of the higher mathematician.

The baroness accepted Wiggins gloomily. When the princess, who had hoped for the Twins, heard that he had been chosen, she accepted him with resignation. Doctor Arbuthnot undertook to arrange the matter.

The disappointed princess informed the Twins of the election of Wiggins; and they cheered her by reporting favorably on the qualifications of their friend, though Erebus said somewhat sadly:

"Of course, he'll insist on being an Indian chief and scalping you; he always does. But you mustn't mind that."

The princess thought that she would not mind it; it would at any rate be a change from listening monotonously to the snores of the baroness.

The Twins found it much more difficult to comfort and cheer their fair-haired, freckled, but infuriated friend. Not only was his reluctance to don the immaculate morning dress of an English young gentleman for the delectation of foreign princesses every whit as sincere as their own, but he felt the invitation to play with a little girl far more insulting than they would have done. They did their best to soothe him and make things pleasant for the princess, pointing out to him the richness of the teas he would assuredly enjoy, and impressing on him the fact that he would be performing a noble charitable action.

"Yes; that's all very well," said Wiggins gloomily. "But I've been seeing ever such a little of you lately in the afternoons; and now I shall see less than ever."

Naturally, he was at first somewhat stiff with the princess; but the stiffness did not last; they became very good active friends; and he scalped her with gratifying frequency. In this way it came about that, in the matter of play, the princess led a double life. She spent the early part of the afternoon in the wood with the Twins; and from tea till the dressing-bell for dinner rang she enjoyed the society of Wiggins. She told no one of her friendship with the Twins; and Wiggins was surprised by her eagerness to hear everything about them he could tell. Between them she was beginning to acquire cheerfulness and muscle; and she was losing her air of delicacy, but not at a rate that satisfied the exigent Terror.

CHAPTER X

AND THE ENTERTAINMENT OF ROYALTY

The time had come for the Twins to take their annual change of air. They took that change at but a short distance from their home, since the cost of a visit to the sea was more than their mother could afford. They were allowed to encamp for ten days, if the weather were fine, in the dry sandstone caves of Deeping Knoll, which rises in the middle of Little Deeping wood, the property of Mr. Anstruther.

Kind-hearted as the Twins were, they felt that to make the journey from the knoll to Muttle Deeping home wood was beyond the bounds of philanthropy; and they broke the news to the princess as gently as they could. She was so deeply grieved to learn that she was no longer going to enjoy their society that, in spite of the fact that she had been made well aware that they despised and abhorred tears, she was presently weeping. She was ashamed; but she could not help it. The compassionate Twins compromised; they promised her that they would try to come every third afternoon; and with that she had to be content.

None the less on the eve of their departure she was deploring bitterly the fact that she would not see them on the morrow, when the Terror was magnificently inspired.

"Look here: why shouldn't you come with us into camp?" he said eagerly. "A week of it would buck you up more than a month at the Grange. You really do get open air camping out at the knoll."

The face of the princess flushed and brightened at the splendid thought. Then it fell; and she said: "They'd never let me—never."

"But you'd never ask them," said the Terror. "You'd just slip away and come with us. We've kept our knowing you so dark that they'd never dream you were with us in the knoll caves."

The princess was charmed, even dazzled, by the glorious prospect. She had come to feel strongly that by far the best part of her life was the afternoons she spent with the Twins in the wood; whole days with them would be beyond the delight of dreams. But to her unadventured soul the difficulties seemed beyond all surmounting. The Twins, however, were used to surmounting difficulties, and at once they began surmounting these.

"The difficult thing is not to get you there, but to keep you there," said the Terror thoughtfully. "You see, I've got to go down every day for milk and things, and they're sure to ask me if I've seen anything of you. Of course, I can't lie about it; and then they'll not only take you away, but they'll probably turn us out of the caves."

"That's the drawback," said Erebus.

The Twins gazed round the wood seeking enlightenment. A deep frown furrowed the Terror's brow; and he said: "If only you weren't a princess they wouldn't make half such a fuss hunting for you, and I might never be asked anything about you."

"I should have to come to the camp incognita, of course," said the princess.

The Terror looked puzzled for a moment; then his face cleared into a glorious smile, and he cried:

"By Jove! Of course you would! I never thought of that! Why, you'd be some one else and not the princess at all! We shouldn't know where the princess was if we were asked."

"Of course we shouldn't!" said Erebus, perceiving the advantage of this ignorance.

"I generally am the Baroness von Zwettel when I travel," said the princess.

The Terror considered the matter, again frowning thoughtfully: "I suppose you have to have a title. But I think an English one would be best here: Lady Rowington now. No one would ever ask us where Lady Rowington is, because there isn't any Lady Rowington."

"Oh, yes: Lady Rowington—I would wish an English title," said the princess readily.

"If we could only think of some way of making them think that she'd been stolen by gipsies, it would be safer still," said Erebus.

"Gipsies don't steal children nowadays," said the Terror; and he paused considering. Then he added, "I tell you what though: Nihilists would—at least they'd steal a princess. Are there any Nihilists in Cassel-Nassau?"

"I never heard of any," said the princess. "There are thousands of Socialists."

"Socialists will do," said the Terror cheerfully.

They were quick in deciding that the princess should not join them till the second night of their stay in camp, to give them time to have everything in order. Then they discussed her needs. She could not bring away with her any clothes, or it would be plain that she had not been stolen. She must share the wardrobe of Erebus.

"But, no. I have money," said the princess, thrusting her hand into her pocket. "Will you not buy me clothes?"

She drew out a little gold chain purse with five sovereigns in it, and handed it to the Terror. He and Erebus examined it with warm admiration, for it was indeed a pretty purse.

"We should have had to buy you a bathing-dress, anyhow. There's a pool just under the knoll," said the Terror. "How much shall we want, Erebus?"

"You'd better have two pounds and be on the safe side," said Erebus.

The Terror transferred two sovereigns from the purse of the princess to his own. Then he arranged that she should meet him outside the door of the peach-garden at nine o'clock, or thereabouts at night. He would wait half an hour that she might not have to hurry and perhaps arouse the suspicion that she had gone of her own free will. He made several suggestions about the manner of her escape.

When she left them, they rode straight to Rowington and set about purchasing her outfit. They bought a short serge skirt, two linen shirts, a blue jersey against the evening chill, a cap, sandals, stockings, underclothing and a bathing-dress. They carried the parcels home on their bicycles. When she saw them on their arrival Mrs. Dangerfield supposed that they were parts of their own equipment.

That evening the Terror worked hard at his ingenious device for throwing the searchers off the scent. It was:

He went to bed much pleased with his handiwork.

They spent a busy morning carrying their camping outfit to Deeping Knoll. The last two hundred yards of path to it was very narrow so that they transported their belongings to the entrance to it in Tom Cobb's donkey-cart, and carried them up to the knoll on their backs.

In other years their outfit had been larger, for their mother had encamped with them. This year she had not cared for the effort; and she had also felt that ten days' holiday out of the strenuous atmosphere which spread itself round the Twins, would be restful and pleasant. She was sure that they might quite safely be trusted to encamp by themselves on Deeping Knoll. Not only were they of approved readiness and resource; but buried in the heart of that wood, they were as safe from the intrusion of evil-doers as on some desert South Sea isle. She was somewhat surprised by the Terror's readiness to take as many blankets as she suggested. In other years he had been disposed to grumble at the number she thought necessary.

The Twins had carried their outfit to the knoll by lunch-time; and they lunched, or rather dined, with a very good appetite. Then they began to arrange their belongings, which they had piled in a heap as they brought them up, in their proper caves. With a break of an hour for a bath this occupied them till tea-time. After tea they bathed again and then set about collecting fuel from the wood. They were too tired to spend much time on cooking their supper; and soon after it, rolled in their blankets on beds of bracken, they were sleeping like logs. They were up betimes, bathing.

This day was far less strenuous than the day before. They spent most of it in the pool or on its bank. In the afternoon Wiggins came and did not leave them till seven. Soon after eight o'clock the Terror set out to keep his tryst with the princess. He took with him the Socialist manifesto and pinned it to the post of a wicket gate opening from the gardens into the park on the opposite side of the Grange to Deeping Knoll. Then he came round to the door in the peach-garden wall two or three minutes before the clock over the stables struck nine.

He had not long to wait; he heard the gentle footfall of the princess on the garden path, the door opened, and she came through it. He shook hands with her warmly; and as they went up the screen of trees she told him how she had bidden the baroness and Miss Lambart good night, gone to her bedroom, ruffled the bed, locked the door, and slipped, unseen, down the stairs and out of the house. He praised her skill; and she found his praise very grateful.

The path to the knoll lay all the way through the dark woods; and the princess found them daunting. They were full of strange noises, many of them eery-sounding; and in the dimness strange terrifying shapes seemed to move. The Terror was not long discovering her fear, and forthwith put his arm round her waist and kept it there wherever the path was broad enough to allow it. When she quivered to some woodland sound, he told her what it was and eased her mind.

She was not strong enough in spite of her exercises and the

Edgar Jepson

active games with Wiggins, to make the whole of the journey over that rough ground at a stretch; and twice when he felt her flagging they sat down and rested. The princess was no longer frightened; she still thrilled to the eeriness of the woods, but she felt quite safe with the Terror. When they rested she snuggled up against him, stared before her into the dark, and thought of all the heroes wandering through the forests of Grimm, with the sense of adventure very strong on her. She was almost sorry when they came at last to the foot of the knoll and saw its top red in the glow of the fire Erebus was keeping bright.

Also Erebus had hot cocoa ready for them; and after her tiring journey the princess found it grateful indeed. They sat for a while in a row before the glowing fire, talking of the Hartz Mountains, which the princess had visited. But soon the yawns which she could not repress showed her hosts how sleepy she was, and the Terror suggested that she should go to bed.

With true courtesy, the Twins had given her the best sleeping-cave to herself, but she displayed such a terrified reluctance to sleep in it alone, that her couch of bracken and her blankets were moved into the cave of Erebus. After the journey and the excitement she was not long falling into a dreamless sleep.

When she awoke next morning, she found the Terror gone to fetch milk. Erebus conducted her down to the pool for her morning bath. The princess did not like it (she had had no experience of cold baths) but under the eye of Erebus she could not shrink; and in she went. She came out shivering, but Erebus helped rub her to a warm glow, and she came to breakfast with such an appetite as she had never before in her life enjoyed.

The knoll was indeed the ideal camping-ground for the romantic; the caves with which it was honeycombed lent themselves to a score of games of adventure; and the princess soon found that she had been called to an active life. It began directly after breakfast with dish-washing; after that she was breathless for an hour in two excited games both of which meant running through the caves and round and over the knoll as hard as you could run and at short intervals yelling as loud as you could yell. After this they put on their bathing-dresses and disported themselves in the pool till it was time to set about the serious business of cooking the dinner, which they took soon after one o'clock.

The Terror kept a careful and protective eye on the princess, helping her, for the most part vigorously, to cover the ground at the required speed. Also he turned her out of the pool, to dry and dress, a full half-hour before he and Erebus left it. After dinner the princess was so sleepy that she could hardly keep her eyes open; and the Terror insisted that she should lie down for an hour. She protested that she did not want to rest, that she did not want to lose a moment of this glorious life; but presently she yielded and was soon asleep.

They were expecting Wiggins in the afternoon. But he could be admitted safely into the secret, since, once he knew that the princess had become Lady Rowington, he would be able with sufficient truthfulness to profess an entire ignorance of her whereabouts. Also he would be very useful, for he could bring them word if suspicion had fallen on them.

At about half past two he arrived, bringing a great tale of the excitement of the countryside at the kidnaping of the princess. So far its simple-minded inhabitants and the suite of the princess were content with the socialist explanation of her disappearance; and three counties round were being searched by active policemen on bicycles for some one who had seen a suspicious motor-car containing Socialists and a princess. It was the general belief that she had been chloroformed and abducted through her bedroom window.

With admirable gravity the Twins discussed with Wiggins the probabilities of their success and of the recovery of the princess, the routes by which the Socialists might have carried her off, and the towns in which the lair to which they had taken her might be. At the end of half an hour of it the princess came out of her cave, her eyes, very bright with sleep, blinking in the sunlight.

Wiggins cried out in surprise; and the Twins laughed joyfully.

Wiggins greeted the princess politely; and then he said reproachfully: "You might have told me that she was coming here."

"You ought to have known as soon as you heard she was missing," said Erebus sternly.

"So I should, if I'd known you knew her at all," said Wiggins.

"That's what nobody knows," said Erebus triumphantly.

"And look here: she's here incognita," said the Terror. "She's taken the traveling name of Lady Rowington; and she's not the princess at all. So if you're asked if the princess is here, you can truthfully say she isn't."

"Of course—I see. This is a go!" said Wiggins cheerfully: and he spurned the earth.

"The only chance of her being found is for somebody to

come up when we're not expecting them and see her," said the Terror. "So I'm going to block the path with thorn-bushes; and any one who comes up it will shout to us. But there's no need to do that yet; nobody will think about us for a day or two."

"No; of course they won't. I didn't," said Wiggins.

The active life persisted throughout that day and the days that followed. It kept the princess always beside the Terror. Always he was using his greater strength to help her lead it at the required speed. Never in the history of the courts of Europe has a princess been so hauled, shoved, dragged, jerked, towed and lugged over rough ground. On the second morning she awoke so stiff that she could hardly move; but by the fifth evening she could give forth an ear-piercing yell that would have done credit to Erebus herself.

All her life the princess had been starved of affection; her mother had died when she was in her cradle; her father had been immersed in his pleasures; no one had been truly fond of her; and she had been truly fond of no one. It is hardly too much to say that she was coming to adore the Terror. Even at their most violent and thrilling moments his care for her never relaxed. He rubbed the ache out of her bruises; he plastered her scratches. He saw to it that she came out of the pool the moment that she looked chill. He picked out for her the tidbits at their meals. He even brushed out her hair, for the thick golden mass was quite beyond the management of the princess; and Erebus firmly refused to play the lady's-maid. Since the Terror was one of those who enjoy doing most things which they are called upon to do, he presently forgot the unmanliness of the occupation, and began to take pleasure in handling the silken strands.

It was on the fifth day, after a bath, when he was brushing

out her hair in the sun on the top of the knoll that he received the severe shock. Heaven knows that the princess was not a demonstrative child; indeed, she had never had the chance. But he had just finished his task and was surveying the shining result with satisfaction, when, of a sudden, without any warning, she threw her arms round his neck and kissed him.

"Oh, you *are* nice!" she said.

The Terror's ineffable serenity was for once scattered to the winds. He flushed and gazed round the wood with horror-stricken eyes: if any one should have seen it!

The princess marked his trouble, and said in a tone of distress: "Don't you like for me to kiss you?"

The Terror swallowed the lump of horror in his throat, and said, faintly but gallantly: "Yes—oh, rather."

"Then kiss me," said the princess simply, snuggling closer to him.

The despairing eyes of the Terror swept the woods; then he kissed her gingerly.

"I *am* fond of you, you know," said the princess in a frankly proprietary tone.

The Terror's scattered wits at last worked. He rose to his feet, and said quickly:

"Yes; let's be getting to the others."

The princess rose obediently.

But the ice was broken; and the kisses of the princess, if not frequent, were, at any rate, not rare. The Terror at first endured them; then he came rather to like them. But he strictly enjoined discretion on her; it would never do for Erebus to learn that she kissed him. The princess had no desire that Erebus, or any one else for that matter, should learn; but discretion and kisses have no natural affinity; and, without their knowing it, Wiggins became aware of the practise.

He had always observed that the Twins had no secrets from each other; and he never dreamed that he was letting an uncommonly awkward cat out of a bag when during a lull in the strenuous life, he said to Erebus:

"I suppose the Terror's in love with the princess, kissing her like that. I think it's awfully silly." And he spurned the earth.

Erebus grabbed his arm and cried fiercely: "He never does!"

Wiggins looked at her in some surprise; her face was one dusky flush; and her eyes were flashing. He had seen her angry often enough, but never so angry as this; and he saw plainly that he had committed a grievous indiscretion.

"Perhaps she kissed him," he said quickly.

"He'd never let her!" cried Erebus fiercely.

"Perhaps they didn't," said Wiggins readily.

"You know they did!" cried Erebus yet more fiercely.

"I may have made a mistake. It's quite easy to make a mistake about that kind of thing," said Wiggins.

Erebus would not have it, and very fiercely she dragged piecemeal from his reluctant lips the story of the surprised idyl. He had seen the princess with an arm round the Terror's neck, and they had kissed.

With clenched fists and blazing eyes Erebus, taking the line of the least resistance, sought the princess. She found her lying back drowsily against a sunny bank.

Erebus came to an abrupt stop before her and cried fiercely: "Princess or no princess, you shan't kiss the Terror!"

The drowsiness fled; and the princess sat up. Her gray eyes darkened and sparkled. She had never made a face in her life; it is not improbable, seeing how sheltered a life she had led, that she was ignorant that faces were made; but quite naturally she made a hideous face at Erebus, and said:

"I shall!"

"If you do, I'll smack you!" cried Erebus; and she ground her teeth.

For all her Hohenzollern blood, the princess was a timid child; but by a gracious provision of nature even the timidest female will fight in the matter of a male. She met Erebus' blazing eyes squarely and said confidently:

"He won't let you. And if you do he'll smack you—much harder!"

Had the princess been standing up, Erebus would have smacked her then and there. But she was sitting safely down; and the Queensberry rules only permit you to strike any one standing up. Erebus forgot them, stooped to strike, remembered them, straightened herself, and with a really pantherous growl dashed away in search of the Terror.

She found him examining and strengthening the barrier of thorns; and she cried:

"I know all about your kissing the princess! I never heard of such silly babyishness!"

It was very seldom, indeed, that the Terror showed himself sensible to the emotions of his sister; but on this occasion he blushed faintly as he said:

"Well, what harm is there in it?"

"It's babyish! It's what mollycoddles do! It's girlish! It's—"

The Terror of a sudden turned brazen; he said loudly and firmly:

"You mind your own business! It isn't babyish at all! She's asked me to marry her; and when we're grown up I'm going to—so there!"

Edgar Jepson

CHAPTER XI

AND THE UNREST CURE

Erebus knew her brother well; she perceived that she was confronted by what she called his obstinacy; and though his brazen-faced admission had raised her to the very height of amazement and horror, she uttered no protest. She knew that protest would be vain, that against his obstinacy she was helpless. She wrung her hands and turned aside into the wood, overwhelmed by his defection from one of their loftiest ideals.

Then followed a period of strain. She assumed an attitude of very haughty contempt toward the errant pair, devoted herself to Wiggins, and let them coldly alone. From this attitude Wiggins was the chief sufferer: the Terror had the princess and the princess had the Terror; Erebus enjoyed her display of haughty contempt, but Wiggins missed the strenuous life, the rushing games, in which you yelled so heartily. As often as he could he stole away from the haughty Erebus and joined the errant pair. It is to be feared that the princess found the kisses sweeter for the ban Erebus had laid on them.

No one in the Deepings suspected that the missing princess was on Deeping Knoll. There had been sporadic outbursts of suspicion that the Twins had had a hand in her disappearance. But no one had any reason to suppose that they and the princess had even been acquainted. Doctor Arbuthnot, indeed, questioned both Wiggins and the Terror; but they were mindful of the fact that Lady Rowington (they were always very careful to address her as Lady Rowington) and not the princess, was at the knoll, and were thus able to assure him with sufficient truthfulness that they could not tell him where the princess was. The bursts of suspicion therefore were brief.

But there was one man in England in whom suspicion had not died down. Suspicion is, indeed, hardly the word for the feeling of Sir Maurice Falconer in the matter. When he first read in his *Morning Post* of the disappearance of the Princess Elizabeth of Cassel-Nassau from Muttle Deeping Grange he said confidently to himself: "The Twins again!" and to that conviction his mind clung.

It was greatly strengthened by a study of the reproduction of the Socialist manifesto on the front page of an enterprising halfpenny paper. He told himself that Socialists are an educated, even over-educated folk, and if one of them did set himself to draw a skull and cross-bones, the drawing would be, if not exquisite, at any rate accurate and unsmudged; that it was highly improbable that a Socialist would spell desperate with two "a's" in an important document without being corrected by a confederate. On the other hand the drawing of the skull and cross-bones seemed to him to display a skill to which the immature genius of the Terror might easily have attained, while he could readily conceive that he would spell desperate with two "a's" in any document.

But Sir Maurice was not a man to interfere lightly in the pleasures of his relations; and he would not have interfered at all had it not been for the international situation produced by the disappearance of the princess. As it was he was so busy with lunches, race meetings, dinners, theater parties, dances and suppers that he was compelled to postpone intervention till the sixth day, when every Socialist organ and organization from San Francisco eastward to Japan was loudly disavowing any connection with the crime, the newspapers of England and Germany were snarling and howling and roaring and bellowing at one another, and the Foreign Office and the German Chancellery were wiring frequent, carefully coded appeals to each other to invent some plausible excuse for not mobilizing their armies and fleets. Even then Sir Maurice, who knew too well the value of German press opinion, would not have interfered, had not the extremely active wife of a cabinet minister consulted him about the easiest way for her to sell twenty thousand pounds' worth of consols. He disliked the lady so strongly that after telling her how she could best compass her design, he felt that the time had come to ease the international situation.

With this end in view he went down to Little Deeping. His conviction that the Twins were responsible for the disappearance of the princess became certitude when he learned from Mrs. Dangerfield that they were encamped on Deeping Knoll, and had been there since the day before that disappearance. But he kept that certitude to himself, since it was his habit to do things in the pleasantest way possible.

He forthwith set out across the fields and walked through the home wood and park to Muttle Deeping Grange. He gave his card to the butler and told him to take it straight to Miss Lambart, with whom he was on terms of friendship rather than of acquaintance; and in less than three minutes she came to him in the drawing-room.

She was looking anxious and worried; and as they shook

hands he said: "Is this business worrying you?"

"It is rather. You see, though the Baroness Von Aschersleben was in charge of the princess, I am partly responsible. Besides, since I'm English, they keep coming to me to have all the steps that are being taken explained; and they want the same explanation over and over again. Since the archduke came it has been very trying. I think that he is more of an imbecile than any royalty I ever met."

"I'm sorry to hear that they've been worrying you like this. If I'd known, I'd have come down and stopped it earlier," said Sir Maurice in a tone of lively self-reproach.

"Stop it? Why, what can you do?" cried Miss Lambart, opening her eyes wide in her surprise.

"Well, I have a strong belief that I could lead you to your missing princess. But it's only a belief, mind. So don't be too hopeful."

Miss Lambart's pretty face flushed with sudden hope:

"Oh, if you could!" she cried.

"Put on your strongest pair of shoes, for I think that it will be rough going part of the way, and order a motor-car, or carriage; if you can, for the easier part; and we'll put my belief to the test," said Sir Maurice briskly.

Miss Lambart frowned, and said in a doubtful tone: "I shan't be able to get a carriage or car without a tiresome fuss. They're very unpleasant people, you know. Could we take the baroness with us? She'll *have* to be carried in something."

"Is she very fat?"

"Very."

"Then she'd never get to the place I have in mind," said Sir Maurice.

"Is it very far? Couldn't we walk to it?"

"It's about three miles," said Sir Maurice.

"Oh, that's nothing—at least not for me. But you?" said Miss Lambart, who had an utterly erroneous belief that Sir Maurice was something of a weakling.

"I can manage it. Your companionship will stimulate my flagging limbs," said Sir Maurice. "Indeed, a real country walk on a warm and pleasant afternoon will be an experience I haven't enjoyed for years."

Miss Lambart was not long getting ready; and they set out across the park toward the knoll which rose, a rounded green lump, above the surface of the distant wood. Sir Maurice had once walked to it with the Twins; and he thought that his memory of the walk helped by a few inquiries of people they met would take him to it on a fairly straight course. It was certainly very pleasant to be walking with such a charming companion through such a charming country.

As soon as they were free of the gardens Miss Lambart said eagerly: "Where are we going to? Where do you think the princess is?"

"You've been here a month. Haven't you heard of the Dangerfield twins?" said Sir Maurice.

"Oh, yes; we were trying to find children to play with the princess; and Doctor Arbuthnot mentioned them. But he said that they were not the kind of children for her, though they were the only high and well-born ones the baroness was clamoring for, in the neighborhood. He seemed to think that they would make her rebellious."

"Then the princess didn't know them?" said Sir Maurice quickly.

"No."

"I wonder," said Sir Maurice skeptically.

"We found a little boy called Rupert Carrington to play with her—a very nice little boy," said Miss Lambart.

"Wiggins! The Twins' greatest friend! Well, I'll be shot!" cried Sir Maurice; and he laughed.

"But do you mean to say that you think that these children have something to do with the princess' disappearance? How old are they?" said Miss Lambart in an incredulous tone, for fixed very firmly in her mind was the belief that the princess had been carried off by the Socialists and foreigners.

"I never know whether they are thirteen or fourteen. But I do know that nothing out of the common happens in the Deepings without their having a hand in it. I have the honor to be their uncle," said Sir Maurice.

"But they'd never be able to persuade her to run away with them. She's a timid child; and she has been coddled and cosseted all her life till she is delicate to fragility," Miss Lambart protested.

"If it came to a matter of persuasion, my nephew would persuade the hind-leg, or perhaps even the fore-leg, off a horse," said Sir Maurice in a tone of deep conviction. "But it would not necessarily be a matter of persuasion."

"But what else could it be—children of thirteen or fourteen!" cried Miss Lambart.

"I assure you that it might quite easily have been force," said Sir Maurice seriously. "My nephew and niece are encamped on Deeping Knoll. It is honeycombed with dry sand-stone caves for the most part communicating with one another. I can conceive of nothing more likely than that the idea of being brigands occurred to one or other of them; and they proceeded to kidnap the princess to hold her for ransom. They might lure her to some distance from the Grange before they had recourse to force."

"It sounds incredible—children," said Miss Lambart.

"Well, we shall see," said Sir Maurice cheerfully. Then he added in a more doubtful tone; "If only we can take them by surprise, which won't be so easy as it sounds."

Miss Lambart feared that they were on a wild goose chase. But it was a very pleasant wild goose chase; she was very well content to be walking with him through this pleasant sunny land. When presently he turned the talk to matters more personal to her, she liked it better still. He was very sympathetic: he sympathized with her in her annoyance at having had to waste so much of the summer on this tiresome *corvee* of acting as lady-in-waiting on the little princess; for, thanks to the domineering jealousy of the baroness, it had been a tiresome *corvee* indeed, instead of the pleasant occupation it might have been. He sympathized with her in her vexation that she had been prevented by that jealousy from improving the health or spirits of the princess.

He was warmly indignant when she told him of the behavior of the baroness and the archduke during the last few days. The baroness had tried to lay the blame of the disappearance of the princess on her; and the archduke, a vast, sun-shaped, billowy mass of fat, infuriated at having been torn from the summer ease of his Schloss to dash to England, had been very rude indeed. She was much pleased by the warmth of Sir Maurice's indignation; but she protested against his making any attempt to punish them, for she did not see how he could do it, without harming himself. But she agreed with him that neither the grand duke, nor the baroness deserved any consideration at her hands.

Their unfailing flow of talk shortened the way; and they soon were in the broad aisle of the wood from which the narrow, thorn-blocked path led to the knoll. Sir Maurice recognized the path; but he did not take it. He knew that the Twins were far too capable not to have it guarded, if the princess were indeed with them. He led the way into the wood on the right of it, and slowly, clearing the way for her carefully, seeing to it that she did not get scratched, or her frock get torn, he brought her in a circuit round to the very back of the knoll.

They made the passage in silence, careful not to tread on a twig, Sir Maurice walking a few feet in front, and all the while peering earnestly ahead through the branches. Now and again a loud yell came from the knoll; and once a chorus of yells. Finding that her coldness (the Terror frankly called it sulking) had no effect whatever on her insensible brother or the insensible princess, Erebus had put it aside; and the strenuous life was once more in full swing.

Once after an uncommonly shrill and piercing yell Miss Lambart said in an astonished whisper:

"That was awfully like the princess' voice."

"I thought you said she was delicate," said Sir Maurice.

"So she was," said Miss Lambart firmly.

Thanks to the careful noiselessness of their approach, they came unseen and unheard to the screen of a clump of hazels at the foot of the knoll, from which they could see the entrance of five caves in its face. They waited, watching it.

It was silent; there was no sign of life; and Sir Maurice was beginning to wonder whether they had, after all, been espied by his keen-eyed kin, when a little girl, with a great plait of very fair hair hanging down her back, came swiftly out of one of the bottom caves and slipped into a clump of bushes to the right of it.

"The princess!" said Miss Lambart; and she was for stepping forward, but Sir Maurice caught her wrist and checked her.

Almost on the instant an amazingly disheveled Wiggins appeared stealing in a crouching attitude toward the entrance to the cave.

"That nice little boy, Rupert Carrington," said Sir Maurice.

Wiggins had almost gained the entrance to the cave when, with an ear-piercing yell, the princess sprang upon him and locked her arms round his neck; they swayed, yelling in anything but unison, and came to the ground.

"Delicate to fragility," muttered Sir Maurice.

"Whatever has she been doing to herself?" said Miss Lambart faintly, gazing at her battling yelling charge with amazed eyes.

"You don't know the Twins," said Sir Maurice.

On his words Erebus came flying down the face of the knoll at a breakneck pace, yelling as she came, and flung herself upon the battling pair. As far as the spectators could judge she and the princess were rending Wiggins limb from limb; and they all three yelled their shrillest. Then with a yell the Terror leaped upon them from the cave and they were all four rolling on the ground while the aching welkin rang.

Suddenly the tangle of whirling limbs was dissolved as Erebus and Wiggins tore themselves free, gained their feet and fled. The princess and the Terror sat up, panting, flushed and disheveled. The princess wriggled close to the Terror, snuggled against him, and put an arm round his neck.

"It was splendid!" she cried, and kissed him.

Unaware of the watching eyes, he submitted to the embrace with a very good grace.

"Well, I never!" said Miss Lambart.

"These delicate children," said Sir Maurice. "But it's certainly a delightful place for lovers. I'm so glad we've found it."

He was looking earnestly at Miss Lambart; and she felt that she was flushing.

"Come along!" she said quickly.

They came out of their clump, about fifteen yards from their quarry.

The quick-eyed Terror saw them first. He did not stir; but a

Edgar Jepson

curious, short, sharp cry came from his throat. It seemed to loose a spring in the princess. She shot to her feet and stood prepared to fly, frowning. The Terror rose more slowly.

"Good afternoon, Highness. I've come to take you back to the Grange," said Miss Lambart.

"I'm not going," said the princess firmly.

"I'm afraid you must. Your father is there; and he wants you," said Miss Lambart.

"No," said the princess yet more firmly; and she took a step sidewise toward the mouth of the cave.

The Terror nodded amiably to his uncle and put his hands in his pockets; he wore the detached air of a spectator.

"But if you don't come of yourself, we shall have to carry you," said Miss Lambart sternly.

The Terror intervened; he said in his most agreeable tone: "I don't see how you can. You can't touch a princess you know. It would be *lese-majeste*. She's told me all about it."

The perplexity spread from the face of Miss Lambart to the face of Sir Maurice Falconer; he smiled appreciatively. But he said: "Oh, come; this won't do, Terror, don't you know! Her highness will *have* to come."

"I don't see how you're going to get her. The only person who could use force is the prince himself, and I don't think he could be got up to the knoll. He's too heavy. I've seen him. And if you did get him up, I don't really think he'd ever find her in these caves," said the Terror in the dispassionate tone of one discussing an entirely impersonal matter.

"Anyhow, I'm not going," said the princess with even greater firmness.

Miss Lambart and Sir Maurice gazed at each other in an equal perplexity.

"You see, there isn't any real reason why she shouldn't stay here," said the Terror. "She came to England to improve her health; and she's improving it ever so much faster here than she did at the Grange. You can *see* how improved it is. She eats nearly as much as Erebus."

"She has certainly changed," said Miss Lambart in a tart tone which showed exactly how little she found it a change for the better.

"The Twins have a transforming effect on the young," said Sir Maurice in a tone of resignation.

"I am much better," said the princess. "I'm getting quite strong, and I can run ever so fast."

She stretched out a tanning leg and surveyed it with an air of satisfaction.

"But it's nonsense!" said Miss Lambart.

"But what can you *do*?" said the Terror gently.

"I'll chance the *lese-majeste*!" cried Miss Lambart; and she sprang swiftly forward.

The princess bolted into the cave and up it. Miss Lambart followed swiftly. The cave ended in a dim passage, ten feet down, the passage forked into three dimmer passages. Miss Lambart stopped short and tried to hear from which of them came the sound of the footfalls of the retiring princess. It came from none of the three; the floor of the eaves was covered with sound-deadening sand. Miss Lambart walked back to the entrance of the cave.

"She has escaped," she said in a tone of resignation.

"Well, I really don't see any reason for you to put yourself about for the sake of that disagreeable crew at the Grange. You have done more than you were called on to do in finding her. You can leave the catching of her to them. There's nothing to worry about: it's quite clear that this camping-out is doing her a world of good," said Sir Maurice in a comforting tone.

"Yes; there is that," said Miss Lambart.

"Let me introduce my nephew. Hyacinth Dangerfield— better, much better, known as the Terror—to you," Said Sir Maurice.

The Terror shook hands with her, and said: "How do you do? I've been wanting to know you: the princess—I mean Lady Rowington—likes you ever so much."

Miss Lambart was appeased.

"Perhaps you could give us some tea? We want it badly," said Sir Maurice.

"Yes, I can. We only drink milk and cocoa, of course. But we have some tea, for Mum walked up to have tea with us yesterday," said the Terror.

"I take it that she saw nothing of the princess," said Sir Maurice.

"Oh, no; she didn't see Lady Rowington. You must remember that she's Lady Rowington here, and not the princess at all," said the Terror.

"Oh? I see now how it was that when you were asked at home, you knew nothing about the princess," said Sir Maurice quickly.

"Yes; that was how," said the Terror blandly.

They had not long to wait for their tea, for the Twins had had their kettle on the fire for some time. Sir Maurice and Miss Lambart enjoyed the picnic greatly. On his suggestion an armistice was proclaimed. Miss Lambart agreed to make no further attempt to capture the princess; and she came out of hiding and took her tea with them.

Miss Lambart was, indeed, pleased with, at any rate, the physical change in the princess, induced by her short stay at the knoll: she was a browner, brighter, stronger child. Plainly, too, she was a more determined child; and while, for her own part, Miss Lambart approved of that change also, she was quite sure that it would not be approved by the princess' kinsfolk and train. But she was somewhat distressed that the legs of the princess should be marred by so many and such deep scratches. She had none of the experienced Twins' quickness to see and dodge thorns. She took Miss Lambart's sympathy lightly enough; indeed she seemed to regard those scratches as scars gained in honorable warfare.

Miss Lambart saw plainly that the billowy archduke would have no little difficulty in recovering her from this fastness; and since she was assured that this green wood life was the very thing the princess needed, she was resolved to give him no help herself. She was pleased to learn that she was in no way responsible for the princess' acquaintance with the

Twins; that she had made their acquaintance and cultivated their society while the careless baroness slept in the peach-garden.

At half past five Sir Maurice and Miss Lambart took their leave of their entertainers and set out through the wood. They had not gone a hundred yards before a splendid yelling informed them that the strenuous life had again begun.

Miss Lambart had supposed that they would return straight to Muttle Deeping Grange with the news of their great discovery. But she found that Sir Maurice had formed other plans. They were both agreed that no consideration was owing to the billowy archduke. His manners deprived him of any right to it. Accordingly, he took her to Little Deeping post-office, and with many appeals to her for suggestions and help wrote two long telegrams. The first was to the editor of the Morning Post, the second was to the prime minister. In both he set forth his discovery of the princess happily encamped with young friends in a wood, and her reasons for running away to them. The postmistress despatched them as he wrote them, that they might reach London and ease the international situation at once. Since both the editor and the prime minister were on friendly and familiar terms with him, there was no fear that the telegrams would fail of their effect.

Then he took Miss Lambart to Colet House, to make the acquaintance of Mrs. Dangerfield, and to inform her how nearly the Twins had plunged Europe into Armageddon. Mrs. Dangerfield received the news with unruffled calm. She showed no surprise at all; she only said that she had found it very strange that a princess should vanish at Muttle Deeping and the Twins have no hand in it. She perceived at once that the princess had quite prevented any disclosure by assuming the name of Lady Rowington.

Miss Lambart found her very charming and attractive, and was in no haste to leave such pleasant companionship for the dull and unpleasant atmosphere of Muttle Deeping Grange. It was past seven therefore when the Little Deeping fly brought her to it; and she went to the archduke with her news.

She found him in the condition of nervous excitement into which he always fell before meals, too excited, indeed, to listen to her with sufficient attention to understand her at the first telling of her news. He was some time understanding it, and longer believing it. It annoyed him greatly. He was taking considerable pleasure in standing on a pedestal before the eyes of Europe as the bereaved Hohenzollern sire. His first, and accurate, feeling was that Europe would laugh consumedly when it learned the truth of the matter. His second feeling was that his noble kinsman, who had been saying wonderful, stirring things about the Terror's manifesto and the stolen princess, would be furiously angry with him.

He began to rave himself, fortunately in his own tongue of which Miss Lambart was ignorant. Then when he grew cooler and paler his oft-repeated phrase was: "Eet must be 'ushed!"

Miss Lambart did not tell him that Sir Maurice had taken every care that the affair should not be hushed up. She did not wish every blow to strike him at once. Then the dinner-bell rang; and in heavy haste he rolled off to the dining-room.

Miss Lambart was betaking herself to her bedroom to dress, when the archduke's equerry, the young mustached Count Zerbst came running up the stairs, bidding her in the name of his master come to dinner at once, as she was. She took no heed of the command, dressed at her ease, and came down just as the archduke, perspiring freely after his struggle with the hors-d'oeuvres, soup and fish, was plunging upon his first entree.

He ate it with great emphasis; and as he ate it he questioned her about the place where his daughter was encamped and the friends she was encamped with. Miss Lambart described the knoll and its position as clearly as she could, and of the Twins she said as little as possible. Then he asked her with considerable acerbity why she had not exercised her authority and brought the princess back with her.

Miss Lambart said that she had no authority over the princess; and that if she had had it, the princess would have disregarded it wholly, and that it was impossible to haul a recalcitrant Hohenzollern through miles of wood by force, since the persons of Hohenzollerns were sacrosanct.

The archduke said that the only thing to do was to go himself and summon home his truant child. Miss Lambart objected that it would mean hewing expensively a path through the wood wide enough to permit his passage, and it was improbable that the owner of the wood would allow it. Thereupon the baroness volunteered to go. Miss Lambart with infinite pleasure explained that for her too an expensive path must be hewn, and went on to declare that if they reached the knoll, there was not the slightest chance of their finding the princess in its caves.

The archduke frowned and grunted fiercely in his perplexity. Then he struck the table and cried:

"Count Zerbst shall do eet! To-morrow morning! You shall 'eem lead to ze wood. 'E shall breeng 'er."

Miss Lambart protested that to wander in the Deeping woods with a German count would hardly be proper.

"Brobare? What ees 'brobare'?" said the archduke.

"*Convenable*," said Miss Lambart.

The archduke protested that such considerations must not be allowed to militate against his being set free to return to Cassel-Nassau at the earliest possible moment. Miss Lambart said that they must. In the end it was decided that a motor-car should be procured from Rowington and that Miss Lambart should guide the archduke and the count to the entrance of the path to the knoll, the count should convey to the princess her father's command to return to the Grange, and if she should refuse to obey, he should haul her by force to the car.

Miss Lambart made no secret of her strong conviction that he would never set eyes, much less hands, on the princess. Count Zerbst's smooth pink face flushed rose-pink all round his fierce little mustache, which in some inexplicable, but unfortunate, fashion accentuated the extraordinary insignificance of his nose; his small eyes sparkled; and he muttered fiercely something about "sdradegy." He looked at Miss Lambart very unamiably. He felt that she was not impressed by him as were the maidens of Cassel-Nassau; and he resented it. He resolved to capture the princess at any cost.

The archduke fumed furiously to find, next morning in the *Morning Post* the true story of his daughter's disappearance; and he was fuming still when the car came from Rowington. It was a powerful car and a weight-carrier; Miss Lambart, who had telephoned for it, had been careful to demand a weight-carrier. With immense fuss the archduke disposed himself in the back of the tonneau which he filled with billowy curves. The moment he was settled in it Miss Lambart sprang to the seat beside the driver, and insisted on keeping it that she might the more easily direct his course.

They were not long reaching the wood; and the chauffeur raised no objection to taking the car up the broad turfed aisle from which ran the path to the knoll. At the entrance of it the count stepped out of the car; and the archduke gave him his final instructions with the air of a Roman father; he was to bring the princess in any fashion, but he was to bring her at once.

In a last generous outburst he cried: "Pooll 'er by the ear! Bud breeng 'er."

The count said that he would, and entered the path with a resolute and martial air. Miss Lambart was not impressed by it. She thought that in his tight-fitting clothes of military cut and his apparently tighter-fitting patent leather boots he looked uncommonly out of place under the green wood trees. She remembered how lightly the Twins and the princess went; and she had the poorest expectation of his getting near any of them. Also, as they had come up the aisle of the woods she had been assailed by a late but serious doubt, whether a weight-carrying motor-car was quite the right kind of vehicle in which to approach the lair of the Twins with hostile intent. Its powerful, loud-throbbing engine had seemed to her to advertise their advent with all the competence of a trumpet.

Her doubt was well-grounded. The quick ears of Erebus were the first to catch its throbbing note, and that while it was still two hundred yards from the entrance of the path to the knoll. Ever since the departure of Miss Lambart and Sir Maurice the Twins had been making ready against invasion, conveying their provisions and belongings to the secret caves.

The secret caves had not been secret before the coming of the Twins to the knoll. They were high up on the outer face of it, airy and well lighted by two inaccessible holes under an overhanging ledge. But the entrance to them was by a narrow shaft which rose sharply from a cave in the heart of the knoll. On this shaft the Twins had spent their best pains for two and a half wet days the year before; and they had reduced some seven or eight feet of it to a passage fifteen inches high and eighteen inches broad. The opening into this passage could, naturally, be closed very easily; and then, in the dim light, it was hard indeed to distinguish it from the wall of the cave. It had been a somewhat difficult task to get their blankets and provisions through so narrow a passage; but it had been finished soon after breakfast.

They were on the alert for invaders; and as soon as they were quite sure that the keen ears of Erebus had made no mistake and that a car was coming up the board aisle, the princess and the Terror squirmed their way up to the secret caves; and Erebus closed the passage behind them, and with small chunks filled in the interstices between the larger pieces of stone so that it looked more than ever a part of the wall of the cave. Then she betook herself to a point of vantage among the bushes on the face of the knoll, from which she could watch the entrance of the path and the coming of the invaders.

The archduke, lying back at his ease in the car, and smoking an excellent cigar, spoke with assurance of catching the one-fifteen train from Rowington to London and the night boat from Dover to Calais. Miss Lambart wasted no breath encouraging him in an expectation based on the efforts of Count Zerbst on the knoll. She stepped out of the car and strolled up and down on the pleasant turf. Presently she saw a figure coming down the aisle from the direction of Little Deeping; when it came nearer, with considerable pleasure she recognized Sir Maurice.

When he came to them she presented him to the archduke as the discoverer of his daughter's hiding-place. The archduke, mindful of the fact that Sir Maurice had given the true story of the disappearance to the world, received him ungraciously. Miss Lambart at once told Sir Maurice of the errand of Count Zerbst and of her very small expectation that anything would come of it. Sir Maurice agreed with her; and the fuming archduke assured them that the count was the most promising soldier in the army of Cassel-Nassau. Then Sir Maurice suggested that they should go to the knoll and help the count. Miss Lambart assented readily; and they set out at once. They skirted the barriers of thorns in the path and came to the knoll. It was quiet and seemed utterly deserted.

They called loudly to the count several times; but he did not answer. Miss Lambart suggested that he was searching the caves and that they should find him and help him search them; they plunged into the caves and began to hunt for him. They did not find the count; neither did they find the princess nor the Twins. They shouted to him many times as they traversed the caves; but they had no answer.

This was not unnatural, seeing that he left the knoll just before they reached it. He had mounted the side of it, calling loudly to the princess. He had gone through half a dozen caves, calling loudly to the princess. No answer had come to his calling. He had kept coming out of the labyrinth on to the side of the knoll. At one of these exits, to his great joy, he had seen the figure of a little girl, dressed in the short serge skirt and blue jersey he had been told the princess was wearing, slipping through the bushes at the foot of the knoll. With a loud shout he had dashed down it in pursuit and plunged after her into the wood. Her sunbonnet was still in sight ahead among the bushes, and by great good fortune he succeeded in keeping it in sight. Once, indeed, when he thought that he had lost it for good and all, it suddenly reappeared ahead of him; and he was able to take up the chase again. But he did not catch her. Indeed he did not lessen the distance between them to an extent appreciable by the naked eye. For a delicate princess she was running with uncommon speed and endurance. Considering his dress and boots and the roughness of the going, he, too, was running with uncommon speed and endurance. It was true that his face was a very bright red and that his so lately stiff, tall, white collar lay limply gray round his neck. But he was not near enough to his quarry to be mortified by seeing that she was but faintly flushed by her efforts and hardly perspiring at all. All the while he was buoyed up by the assurance that he would catch her in the course of the next hundred yards.

Then his quarry left the wood, by an exceedingly small gap, and ran down a field path toward the village of Little Deeping. By the time the count was through the gap she had a lead of a hundred yards. To his joy, in the open country, on the smoother path, he made up the lost ground quickly. When they reached the common, he was a bare forty yards behind her. He was not surprised when in despair she left the path and bolted into the refuge of an old house that stood beside it.

Mopping his hot wet brow he walked up the garden path with a victorious air, and knocked firmly on the door. Sarah opened it; and he demanded the instant surrender of the princess. Sarah heard him with an exasperating air of blank bewilderment. He repeated his demand more firmly and loudly.

Sarah called to Mrs. Dangerfield: "Please, mum: 'ere's a furrin gentleman asking for a princess. I expect as it's that there missing one."

"Do nod mock! She 'ees 'ere!" cried the count fiercely.

Then Mrs. Dangerfield came out of the dining-room where she had been arranging flowers, and came to the door.

"The princess is not here," she said gently.

"But I haf zeen 'er! She haf now ad once coom! She 'ides!" cried the count.

At that moment Erebus came down the hall airily swinging her sunbonnet by its strings. The eyes of the count opened wide; so did his mouth.

"I expect he means me. At least he's run after me all the way from the knoll here," said Erebus in a clear quiet voice.

The count's eyes returned to their sockets; and he had a sudden outburst of fluent German. He did not think that any of his hearers could understand that portion of his native tongue he was using; he hoped they could not; he could not help it if they did.

Mrs. Dangerfield looked from him to Erebus thoughtfully. She did not suppose for a moment that it was mere accident that had caused the count to take so much violent exercise on such a hot day. She was sorry for him. He looked so fierce and young and inexperienced to fall foul of the Twins.

Erebus caught her mother's thoughtful eye. At once she cried resentfully: "How could I possibly tell it was the sunbonnet which made him think I was the princess? He never asked me who I was. He just shouted once and ran after me. I was hurrying home to get some salad oil and get back to the knoll by lunch."

"Yes, you would run all the way," said Mrs. Dangerfield patiently.

"Well, you'd have run, too, Mum, with a foreigner running after you! Just look at that mustache! It would frighten anybody!" cried Erebus in the tone of one deeply aggrieved by unjust injurious suspicions.

"Yes, I see," said her mother with undiminished patience.

She invited the count to come in and rest and get cool; and she allayed his fine thirst with a long and very grateful whisky and soda. He explained to her at length, three times, how he had come to mistake Erebus for the flying princess, for he was exceedingly anxious not to appear foolish in the eyes of such a pretty woman. Erebus left them together; she made a point of taking a small bottle of salad oil to the knoll. They had no use for salad oil indeed; but it had been an afterthought, and she owed it to her conscience to take it. That would be the safe course.

In the meantime the archduke was sitting impatiently in the car, looking frequently at his watch. He had expected the count to return with the princess in, at the longest, a quarter of an hour. Then he had expected Miss Lambart and Sir Maurice to return with the count and the princess in, at the longest, a quarter of an hour. None of them returned. The princess was sitting on a heap of bracken in the highest of the secret caves, and the Terror was taking advantage of this enforced quiet retirement to brush out her hair. The count sat drinking whisky and soda and explained to Mrs. Dangerfield that he had not really been deceived by the sunbonnet and that he was very pleased that he had been deceived by it, since it had given him the pleasure of her acquaintance. Miss Lambart and Sir Maurice sat on a bank and talked seriously about everything and certain other things, but chiefly about themselves and each other.

So the world wagged as the archduke saw the golden minutes which lay between him and the one-fifteen slipping away while his daughter remained uncaught. He chafed and fumed. His vexation grew even more keen when he came to the end of his cigar and found that the thoughtless count had borne away the case. He appealed to the chauffeur for advice; but the chauffeur, a native of Rowington and ignorant of Beaumarchais, could give him none.

At half past twelve the archduke rose to his full height in the car, bellowed: "Zerbst! Zerbst! Zerbst!" and sank down again panting with the effort.

The chauffeur looked at him with compassionate eyes. The archduke's bellow, for all his huge round bulk, was but a thin and reedy cry. No answer came to it; no one came from the path to the knoll.

"P'raps if I was to give him a call, your Grace," said the chauffeur, somewhat complacent at displaying his knowledge of the right way to address an archduke.

"Yes, shout!" said the archduke quickly.

The chauffeur rose to his full height in the car and bellowed: "Zerbst! Zerbst! Zerbst!"

No answer came to the call; no one came from the path to the knoll.

In three minutes the archduke was grinding his teeth in a black fury.

Then with an air of inspiration he cried: "I shout—you

shout—all ad vonce!"

"Every little 'elps," said the chauffeur politely.

With that they both rose to their full height in the car and together bellowed: "Zerbst! Zerbst! Zerbst!"

No answer came to it; no one came from the path to the knoll.

On his sunny bank on the side of the knoll Sir Maurice said carelessly: "He seems to be growing impatient."

"He isn't calling us. And it's no use our going back without either the princess or the count," said Miss Lambart quickly.

"Not the slightest," said Sir Maurice; and he drew her closer, if that were possible, to him and kissed her.

To this point had their cooperation in the search for the princess and their discussion of everything and certain other things ripened their earlier friendship. They, or rather Sir Maurice, had even been discussing the matter of being married at an early date.

"I don't think I shall let you go back to the Grange at all. They don't treat you decently, you know—not even for royalties," he went on.

"Oh, it wouldn't do not to go back—at any rate for to-night—though, of course, there's no point in my staying longer, since the princess isn't there," said Miss Lambart.

"You don't know: perhaps Zerbst has caught her by now and is hauling her to her circular sire," said Sir Maurice. "The Twins can not be successful all the time."

"We ought to go and search those caves thoroughly," said Miss Lambart.

"That wouldn't be the slightest use," said Sir Maurice in a tone of complete certainty. "If the princess is in the caves, she is not in an accessible one. But as a matter of fact she is quite as likely, or even likelier, to be at the Grange. The Twins are quite intelligent enough to hide princesses in the last place you would be likely to look for them. It's no use our worrying ourselves about her; besides, we're very comfortable here. Why not stay just as we are?"

They stayed there.

But the archduke's impatience was slowly rising to a fury as the minutes that separated him from the one-fifteen slipped away. At ten minutes to one he was seized by a sudden fresh fear lest the searchers should be so long returning as to make him late for lunch; and at once he despatched the chauffeur to find them and bring them without delay.

The chauffeur made no haste about it. He had heard of the caves on Deeping Knoll and had always been curious to see them. Besides, he made it a point of honor not to smoke on duty; he had not had a pipe in his mouth since eleven o'clock; and he felt now off duty. He explored half a dozen caves thoroughly before he came upon Miss Lambart and Sir Maurice and gave them the archduke's message. They joined him in his search for Count Zerbst, going through the caves and calling to him loudly.

The one-fifteen had gone; and the hour of lunch was perilously near. The face of the archduke was dark with the dread that he would be late for it. There was a terrifying but sympathetic throbbing not far from his solar plexus.

Every two or three minutes he rose to his full height in the car and bellowed: "Zerbst! Zerbst! Zerbst!"

Still no answer came to the call; no one came from the path to the knoll.

Then at the very moment at which on more fortunate days he was wont to sink heavily, with his mouth watering, into a large chair before a gloriously spread German table, he heard the sound of voices; and the chauffeur, Miss Lambart and Sir Maurice came out of the path to the knoll.

They told the duke that they had neither seen nor heard anything of the princess, her hosts, or Count Zerbst. The archduke cursed his equerry wheezily but in the German tongue, and bade the chauffeur get into the car and drive to the Grange as fast as petrol could take him.

Sir Maurice bade Miss Lambart good-by, saluted the archduke, and the car went bumping down the turfed aisle. Once in the road the chauffeur, anxious to make trial at an early moment of the archducal hospitality, let her rip. But half a mile down the road, they came upon a slow-going, limping wayfarer. It was Count Zerbst. After a long discussion with Mrs. Dangerfield he had decided that since Erebus had slipped away back to the knoll, it would be impossible for him to find his way to it unguided; and he had set out for Muttle Deeping Grange. In the course of his chase of Erebus and his walk back his patent leather boots had found him out with great severity; and he was indeed footsore. He stepped into the grateful car with a deep sigh of relief.

A depressed party gathered round the luncheon table; Miss Lambart alone was cheerful. The archduke had been much shaken by his terrors and disappointments of the morning.

Edgar Jepson

Count Zerbst had acquired a deep respect for the intelligence of the young friends of the princess; and he had learned from Mrs. Dangerfield, who had discussed the matter with Sir Maurice, that since her stay at the knoll was doing the princess good, and was certainly better for her than life with the crimson baroness at the Grange, she was not going to annoy and discourage her charitable offspring by interfering in their good work for trivial social reasons. The baroness was bitterly angry at their failure to recover her lost charge.

They discussed the further measures to be taken, the archduke and the baroness with asperity, Count Zerbst gloomily. He made no secret of the fact that he believed that, if he dressed for the chase and took to the woods, he would in the end find and capture the princess, but it might take a week or ten days. The archduke cried shame upon a strategist of his ability that he should be baffled by children for a week or ten days. Count Zerbst said sulkily that it was not the children who would baffle him, but the caves and the woods they were using. At last they began to discuss the measure of summoning to their aid the local police; and for some time debated whether it was worth the risk of the ridicule it might bring upon them.

Miss Lambart had listened to them with distrait ears since she had something more pleasant to give her mind to. But at last she said with some impatience: "Why can't the princess stay where she is? That open-air life, day and night, is doing her a world of good. She is eating lots of good food and taking ten times as much exercise as ever she took in her life before."

"Eembossible! Shall I live in a cave?" cried the baroness.

"It doesn't matter at all where you live. It is the princess we are considering," said Miss Lambart unkindly, for she had come quite to the end of her patience with the baroness.

"Drue!" said the archduke quickly.

"Shall eet zen be zat ze princess live ze life of a beast in a gave?" cried the baroness.

"She isn't," said Miss Lambart shortly. "In fact she's leading a far better and healthier and more intelligent life than she does here. The doctor's orders were never properly carried out."

"Ees zat zo?" said the archduke, frowning at the baroness.

"Eengleesh doctors! What zey know? Modern!" cried the baroness scornfully.

In loud and angry German the archduke fell furiously upon the baroness, upbraiding her for her disobedience of his orders. The baroness defended herself loudly, alleging that the princess would by now be dying of a galloping consumption had she had all the air and water the doctors had ordered her. But the archduke stormed on. At last he had some one on whom he could vent his anger with an excellent show of reason; and he vented it.

Presently, for the sake of Miss Lambart's counsel in the matter, they returned to the English tongue and discussed seriously the matter of the princess remaining at the knoll. They found many objections to it, and the chief of them was that it was not safe for three children to be encamped by themselves in the heart of a wood.

Miss Lambart grew tired of assuring them that the Twins were more efficient persons than nine Germans out of ten; and at last she said:

"Well, Highness, to set your fears quite at rest, I will go and stay at the knoll myself. Then you can go back to Cassel-Nassau with your mind at ease; and I will undertake that the princess comes to you in better health than if she had stayed on here."

"Bud 'ow would she be zafer wiz a young woman, ignorant and—" cried the baroness, furious at this attempt to usurp her authority.

"Goot!" cried the archduke cutting her short; and his face beamed at the thought of escaping forthwith to his home. "Eet shall be zo! And ze baroness shall go alzo to Cassel-Nassau zo zoon az I zend a lady who do as ze doctors zay."

So it was settled; and Miss Lambart was busy for an hour collecting provisions, arranging that fresh provisions should be brought to the path to the knoll every morning and preparing and packing the fewest possible number of garments she would need during her stay.

Then she bade the relieved archduke good-by; and set out in the Rowington car to the knoll. Not far from the park gates she met Sir Maurice strolling toward the Grange, and took him with her. At the entrance of the path to the knoll they took the baskets of provisions and Miss Lambart's trunk from the car, and dismissed it. Then they went to the knoll.

It was silent; there were no signs of the presence of man about it. But after Sir Maurice had shouted three times that they came in peace-bearing terms, Erebus and Wiggins came out of one of the caves above them and heard the news. She made haste to bear it to the Terror and the princess who received it with joy. They had already been cooped up long enough in the secret caves and were eager to plunge once more into the strenuous life. They welcomed Miss Lambart warmly; and the princess was indeed pleased to have her fears removed and her position at the knoll secure.

They made Miss Lambart one of themselves and admitted her to a full share of the strenuous life. She played her part in it manfully. Even Erebus, who was inclined to carp at female attainments, was forced to admit that as a brigand, an outlaw, or a pirate she often shone.

But Sir Maurice, who was naturally a frequent visitor, never caught her engaged in the strenuous life. Indeed, on his arrival she disappeared; and always spent some minutes after his arrival removing traces of the speed at which she had been living it, and on cooling down to life on the lower place. Both of them found the knoll a delightful place for lovers.

CHAPTER XII

AND THE MUTTLE DEEPING FISHING

Since the strenuous life was found to be so strengthening to the princess, the Twins stayed in camp a week longer than had been in the beginning arranged. Thrown into such intimate relations with Miss Lambart, it was only natural that they should grow very friendly with her. It was therefore a bitter blow to Erebus to find that she was not only engaged to their Uncle Maurice but also about to be married to him in the course of the next few weeks. She grumbled about it to the Terror and did not hesitate to assert that his bad example in the matter of the princess had put the idea of love-making into these older heads. Then, in a heart to heart talk, she strove earnestly with Miss Lambart, making every effort to convince her that love and marriage were very silly things, quite unworthy of those who led the strenuous life. She failed. Then she tried to persuade Sir Maurice of that plain fact, and failed again. He declared that it was his first duty, as an uncle, to be married before his nephew, and that if he were not quick about it the Terror would certainly anticipate him. Erebus carried his defense to the Terror with an air of bitter triumph; and there was a touch of disgusted misanthropy in her manner for several days. The princess on the other hand found the engagement the most natural and satisfactory thing in the world. Her only complaint was that she and the Terror were not old enough to be married on the same day as Miss Lambart.

Probably Miss Lambart and Sir Maurice enjoyed the life at the knoll even more than the children, for the felicity of lovers is the highest felicity, and the knoll is the ideal place for them. Sir Maurice arrived at it not so very much later, considering his urban habit, than sunrise; and he did not leave it till long after sunset. But the pleasantest days will come to an end; and the camp was broken up, since the archduke's tenancy of the Grange expired, and the princess must return to Germany. She was bitterly grieved at parting with the Terror, and assured him that she would certainly come to England the next summer, or even earlier, perhaps at Christmas, to see him again. It seemed not unlikely that after her short but impressive association with the Twins she would have her way about it. Nevertheless, in spite of her exhaustive experience of the strenuous life, and of the firm ideals of those who led it, at their parting she cried in the most unaffected fashion.

Soon after her departure from the Grange the Twins learned that Sir James Morgan, its owner, had returned from Africa, where he had for years been hunting big game, and proposed to live at Muttle Deeping, at any rate for a while. It had always been their keen desire to fish the Grange water, for it had been carefully preserved and little fished all the years Sir James had been wandering about the world. But Mr. Hilton, the steward of the Grange estate, had always refused their request. He believed that their presence would be good neither for the stream, the fish, nor the estate.

But now that they were no longer dealing with an underling whom they felt to be prejudiced, but with the owner himself, they thought that they might be able to compass their desire. Also they felt that the sooner they made the attempt to do so the better: Sir James might hear unfavorable accounts of them, if they gave him time to consort freely with his neighbors. Therefore, with the help of their literary mainstay, Wiggins, they composed a honeyed letter to him, asking leave to fish the Grange water. Sir James consulted Mr. Hilton about the letter, received an account of the Twins from him which made him loath indeed to give them leave; and since he had used a pen so little for so many years that it had become distasteful to him to use it at all, he left their honeyed missive unanswered.

The Twins waited patiently for an answer for several days. Then it was slowly borne in upon them that Sir James did not mean to answer their letter at all; and they grew very angry indeed. Their anger was in close proportion to the pains they had spent on the letter. The name of Sir James was added to the list of proscribed persons they carried in their retentive minds.

It did not seem likely that they would get any chance of punishing him for the affront he had put on them. Scorching, in his feverish, Central African way, along the road to Rowington in a very powerful motor-car, he looked well beyond their reach. But Fortune favors the industrious who watch their chances; and one evening Erebus came bicycling swiftly up to the cats' home, and cried:

"As I came over Long Ridge I saw Sir James Morgan poaching old Glazebrook's water!"

The Terror did not cease from carefully considering the kitten in his hands, for he was making a selection to send to Rowington market.

"Are you sure?" he said calmly. "It's a long way from the ridge to the stream."

"Not for my eyes!" said Erebus with some measure of impatience in her tone. "I'm quite sure that it was Sir James; and I'm quite sure that it was old Glazebrook's meadow. Lend me your handkerchief."

The handkerchief that the Terror lent her might have easily been of a less pronounced gray; but Erebus mopped her beaded brow with it in a perfect content. She had ridden home as fast as she could ride with her interesting news.

"I wish I'd seen him too," said the Terror thoughtfully.

"It's quite enough for me to have seen him!" said Erebus with some heat.

"It would be better if we'd both seen him," said the Terror firmly.

"It's such beastly cheek his poaching himself after taking no notice of our letter!" said Erebus indignantly.

"Yes, it is," said the Terror.

She went on to set forth the enormity of the conduct of their neighbor at considerable length. The Terror said nothing; he did not look to be listening to her. In truth he was considering what advantage might be drawn from Sir James' transgression.

At last he said: "The first thing to do is for both of us to catch him poaching."

Erebus protested; but the Terror carried his point, with the result that two evenings later they were in the wood above the trout-stream, stretched at full length in the bracken, peering through the hedge of the wood at Sir James Morgan

Edgar Jepson

so patiently and vainly fishing the stream below.

"He'll soon be at the boundary fence," said the Terror in a hushed voice of quiet satisfaction.

"If only he goes on catching nothing on this side of it!" said Erebus who kept wriggling in a nervous impatience.

"It's on the other side of it they're rising," said the Terror in a calmly hopeful tone.

Sir James, unconscious of those eagerly gazing eyes, made vain cast after vain cast. He was a big game hunter; he had given but little time and pains to this milder sport; and he came to the fence at which his water ceased and that of Mr. Glazebrook began, with his basket still empty of trout. He looked longingly at his neighbor's water; as the Terror had said, the trout in it were rising freely. Then the watchers saw him shrug his shoulders and turn back.

"He's not going to poach, after all!" cried Erebus in a tone of acute disappointment.

"Look here: are you really quite sure you saw him poaching at all? Long Ridge is a good way off," said the Terror looking across to it.

"I did. I tell you he was half-way down old Glazebrook's meadow," said Erebus firmly.

"It's very disappointing," said the Terror, frowning at the disobliging fisherman; then he added with philosophic calm: "Well, it can't be helped; we've got to go on watching him every evening till he does. If he's poached once, he'll poach again."

"Look!" said Erebus, gripping his arm.

Sir James had stopped fishing and was walking back to the boundary fence. He stood for a while beside the gap in it, hesitating, scanning the little valley down which the stream ran, with his keen hunter's eyes. It is to be feared that he had been too long used to the high-handed methods that prevail in the ends of the earth where big game dwell, to have a proper sense of the sanctity of his neighbor's fish. Moreover, Mr. Glazebrook was guilty of the practise of netting his water and sending the trout, alive in cans, to a London restaurant. Sir James felt strongly that it was his duty as a sportsman to give them the chance of making a sports-manlike end.

But Mr. Glazebrook was an uncommonly disagreeable man; and since Glazebrook farm marched with the western meadows of the Morgans, the Morgans and the Glazebrooks had been at loggerheads for at least fifty years. Assuredly the farmer would prosecute Sir James, if he caught him poaching.

Yet the valley and the meadows down the stream were empty of human beings; and as for the wood, there would be no one but his own keeper in the wood. Doubtless that keeper would, from the abstract point of view, regard poaching with abhorrence. But he would perceive that his master was doing a real kindness to the Glazebrook trout by giving them that chance of making a sportsman-like end. At any rate the keeper would hold his tongue.

Sir James climbed through the gap.

The Twins breathed a simultaneous sigh of relief; and Erebus said in a tone of triumph: "Well, he's gone and done it now."

"Yes, we've got him all right," said the Terror in a tone of calm thankfulness.

Fortune favored the unscrupulous; and in the next forty minutes Sir James caught three good fish.

He had just landed the third when the keen eyes of Erebus espied a figure coming up the bank of the stream two meadows away.

"Look! There's old Glazebrook! He'll catch him! Won't it be fun?" she cried, wriggling in her joy.

The Terror gazed thoughtfully at the approaching figure; then he said: "Yes: it would be fun. There'd be no end of a row. But it wouldn't be any use to us. I'm going to warn him."

With that he sent a clear cry of "Cave!" ringing down the stream.

In ten seconds Sir James was back on his own land.

The Twins crawled through the bracken to a narrow path, went swiftly and noiselessly down it, and through a little gate on to the high road.

As he set foot on it the Terror said with cold vindictiveness: "We'll teach him not to answer our letters."

He climbed over a gate into a meadow on the other side of the road, took their bicycles one after the other from behind the hedge, and lifted them over the gate. They reached home in time for dinner.

During the meal Mrs. Dangerfield asked how they had been

spending the time since tea; and the Terror said, quite truth-fully, that they had been for a bicycle ride. She did not press him to be more particular in his account of their doings, though from Erebus' air of subdued excitement and expec-tancy she was aware that some important enterprise was in hand; she had no desire to put any strain on the Terror's uncommon power of polite evasion.

She was not at all surprised when, at nine o'clock, she went out into the garden and called to them that it was bedtime, to find that they were not within hearing. She told herself that she would be lucky if she got them to bed by ten. But she would have been surprised, indeed, had she seen them, half an hour earlier, slip out of the back door, in a condition of exemplary tidiness, dressed in their Sunday best.

They wheeled their bicycles out of the cats' home quietly, mounted, rode quickly down the road till they were out of hearing of the house, and then slackened their pace in order to reach their destination cool and tidy. They timed their arrival with such nicety that as they dismounted before the door of Deeping Hall, Sir James Morgan, in the content inspired by an excellent dinner, was settling himself comfortably in an easy chair in his smoking-room.

They mounted the steps of the Court without a tremor: they were not only assured of the justice of their cause, they were assured that it would prevail. A landed proprietor who preserves his pheasants and his fish with the usual strictness, *can not* allow himself to be prosecuted for poaching.

The Terror rang the bell firmly; and Mawley, the butler, surprised at the coming of visitors at so late an hour, opened the door himself.

"Good evening, Mr. Mawley, we want to see Sir James on

　　　　　　Edgar Jepson

important business," said the Terror with a truly businesslike air.

Mawley had come to the Grange in the train of the Princess Elizabeth; and since he found the Deeping air uncommonly bracing, he had permitted Sir James to keep him on at the Grange after her return to Cassel-Nassau. He had made the acquaintance of the Twins during the last days of her stay, after the camp had been broken up, and had formed a high opinion of their ability and their manners. Moreover, of a very susceptible nature, he had a warm admiration of Mrs. Dangerfield whom he saw every Sunday at Little Deeping church.

None the less he looked at them doubtfully, and said in a reproachful tone: "It's very late, Master Terror. You can't expect Sir James to see people at this hour."

"I know it's late; but the business is important—very important," said the Terror firmly.

Mawley hesitated. His admiration of Mrs. Dangerfield made him desirous of obliging her children. Then he said:

"If you'll sit down a minute, I'll tell Sir James that you're here."

"Thank you," said the Terror; and he and Erebus came into the great hall, sat down on a couch covered by a large bearskin, and gazed round them at the arms and armor with appreciative eyes.

Mawley found Sir James lighting a big cigar; and told him that Master and Miss Dangerfield wished to see him on business.

"Oh? They're the two children who wrote and asked me for leave to fish. But Hilton told me that they were the most mischievous little devils in the county, so I took no notice of their letter," said Sir James.

"Well, being your steward, Sir James, Mr. Hilton would be bound to tell you so. But it's my belief that, having the name for it, a lot of mischief is put down to them which they never do. And after all they're Dangerfields, Sir James; and you couldn't expect them to behave like ordinary children," said Mawley in the tone and manner of a persuasive diplomat.

"Well, I don't see myself giving them leave to fish," said Sir James. "There are none too many fish in the stream as it is; and a couple of noisy children won't make those easier to catch. But I may as well tell them so myself; so you may bring them here."

Mawley fetched the Twins and ushered them into the smoking-room. They entered it with the self-possessed air of persons quite sure of themselves, and greeted Sir James politely.

He was somewhat taken aback by their appearance and air, for his steward had somehow given him the impression that they were thick, red-faced and robustious. He felt that these pleasant-looking young gentlefolk could never have really earned their unfortunate reputation. There must be a mistake somewhere.

The Twins were, on their part also, far more favorably impressed by him than they had looked to be; his lean tanned face, with the rather large arched nose, the thin-lipped melancholy mouth, not at all hidden by the small clipped mustache, and his keen eyes, almost as blue as those of the Terror, pleased them. He looked an uncommonly

Edgar Jepson

dependable baronet.

"Well, and what is this important matter you wished to see me about?" he said in a more indulgent tone than he had expected to use.

"We saw you in Glazebrook's meadow this afternoon—poaching," said the Terror in a gentle, almost deprecatory tone.

Sir James sat rather more upright in his chair, with a sudden sense of discomfort. He had not connected this visit with his transgression.

"And you caught three fish," said Erebus in a sterner voice.

"Oh? Then it was one of you who called 'Cave!' from the wood?" said Sir James.

"Yes; we didn't want old Glazebrook to catch you," said the Terror.

"Oh—er—thanks," said Sir James in a tone of discomfort.

"That wouldn't have been any use to us," said the Terror.

"Of use to you?" said Sir James.

"Yes; if he'd caught you, there wouldn't be any reason why we should fish your water," said the Terror.

Sir James looked puzzled:

"But is there any reason now?" he said.

"Yes. You see, you were poaching," said the Terror in a very gentle explanatory voice.

"And you caught three fish," said Erebus in something of the manner of a chorus in an Athenian tragedy.

Sir James sat bolt upright with a sudden air of astonished enlightenment:

"Well, I'm—hanged if it isn't blackmail!" he cried.

"Blackmail?" said the Terror in a tone of pleasant animation. "Why, that's what the Scotch reavers used to do! I never knew exactly what it was."

"And we're doing it. That is nice," said Erebus, almost preening herself.

"But this is disgraceful! If you'd been village children—but gentlefolk!" cried Sir James with considerable heat.

"Well, the Douglases were gentlefolk; and they blackmailed," said the Terror in a tone of sweet reason.

"Poaching's a misdemeanor; blackmailing's a kind of stealing," said Erebus virtuously, forgetting for the moment her mother's fur stole.

"Poaching's a misdemeanor; blackmailing's a felony," said Sir James loftily.

The distinction was lost on the Twins; and Erebus said with conviction: "Poaching's worse."

Sir James hated to be beaten; and he looked from one to the other with very angry eyes. The Twins wore a cold imperturbable air. Their appearance no longer pleased him.

"It's your own fault entirely," said the Terror coldly. "If you'd been civil and answered our letter, even refusing, we shouldn't have bothered about you. But you didn't take any notice of it—"

"And it was beastly cheek," said Erebus.

"You couldn't expect us to stand that kind of thing. So we kept an eye on you and caught you poaching," said the Terror.

"Without any excuse for it. You've plenty of fishing of your own," said Erebus severely.

"And if I don't give you leave to fish my water, you're going to sneak to the police, are you?" said Sir James in a tone of angry disgust.

The Terror flushed and with a very cold dignity said: "We aren't going to do anything of the kind; and we don't want any leave to fish your water at all. We're just going to fish it; and if you go sneaking to the police and prosecuting us, then after you've started it you'll get prosecuted yourself by old Glazebrook. That's what we came to say."

"And that'll teach you to be polite and answer people next time they write to you," said Erebus in a tone of cold triumph.

On her words they rose; and while Sir James was struggling furiously to find words suitable to their tender years, they bade him a polite good night, and left the room.

Their departure was a relief; Sir James rose hastily to his feet and expressed his feelings without difficulty. Then he began to laugh. It was rather on the wrong side of his face; and the knowledge that he had been worsted in his own smoking-room, and that by two children, rankled. He was not used to being worsted, even in the heart of Africa, by much more ferocious creatures. But after sleeping on the matter, he perceived yet more clearly that they had him, as he phrased it, in a cleft stick; and he told his head-keeper that the Dangerfield children were allowed to fish his water.

Edgar Jepson

CHAPTER XIII

AND AN APOLOGY

The vindication of their dignity filled the Twins with a cold undated triumph; but they enjoyed the liveliest satisfaction in being able to fish in well-stocked water, because the trout tempted their mother's faint appetite.

She had grown stronger during the summer. She was not, indeed, definitely ill; she was not even definitely weak. But, a woman of spirit and intelligence, she was suffering from the wearisome emptiness of her life in the country. It was sapping her strength and energy; in it she would grow old long before her time. The Twins had been used to find her livelier and more spirited, keenly interested in their doings; and the change troubled them. Doctor Arbuthnot prescribed a tonic for her; and now and again, as in the matter of the peaches and now of the trout, they set themselves to procure some delicacy for her. But she made no real improvement; and the empty country life was poisoning the springs of her being.

Sir James had expected to be annoyed frequently by the sight and sound of the Twins on the bank of the stream. To his pleased surprise he neither saw nor heard them. For the most part they fished in the early morning and brought their catch home to tempt their mother's appetite at breakfast. But if they did fish in the evening, one or the other acted as scout, watching Sir James' movements; and they kept out of his sight. They had gained their end; and their natural delicacy assured them that the sight of them could not be pleasant to Sir James. As the Terror phrased it:

"He must be pretty sick at getting a lesson; and there's no point in rubbing it in."

Then one evening (by no fault of theirs) he came upon them. Erebus was playing a big trout; and she had no thought of abandoning it to spare Sir James' feelings. Besides, if she had had such a thought, it was impracticable, since Mrs. Dangerfield had come with them.

He watched Erebus play her fish for two or three minutes; then it snapped the gut and was gone.

"Evidently you're no so good at fishing as blackmailing," said Sir James in a nasty carping tone, for the fact that they had worsted him still rankled in his heart.

"I catch more fish than you do, anyhow!" said Erebus with some heat; and she cast an uneasy glance over his shoulder.

Sir James turned to see what she had glanced at and found himself looking into the deep brown eyes of a very pretty woman.

He had not seen her when he had come out of the bushes on to the scene of the struggle; he had been too deeply interested in it to remove his eyes from it; and she had watched it from behind him.

"This is Sir James Morgan, mother," said the Terror quickly.

Sir James raised his cap; Mrs. Dangerfield bowed, and said gratefully: "It was very good of you to give my children leave to fish."

"Oh—ah—yes—n-n-not at all," stammered Sir James, blushing faintly.

He was unused to women and found her presence confusing.

"Oh, but it was," said Mrs. Dangerfield. "And I'm seeing that they don't take an unfair advantage of your kindness, for they told me that, thanks to Mr. Glazebrook's netting his part of it, there are none too many fish in the stream."

"It's very good of you. B-b-but I don't mind how many they catch," said Sir James.

He shuffled his feet and gazed rather wildly round him, for he wished to remove himself swiftly from her disturbing presence. Yet he did not wish to; he found her voice as charming as her eyes.

Mrs. Dangerfield laughed gently, and said: "You would, if I let them catch as many as they'd like to."

"Are they as good fishermen as that?" said Sir James.

"Well, they've been fishing ever since they could handle a rod. They are supposed to empty the free water by Little Deeping Village every spring. So I limit them to three fish a day," said Mrs. Dangerfield; and there was a ring of motherly pride in her voice which pleased him.

"It's very good of you," said Sir James. He hesitated, shuffled his feet again, took a step to go; then looking rather earnestly at Mrs. Dangerfield, he added in a rather uncertain voice: "I should like to stay and see how they do it. I might pick up a wrinkle or two."

"Of course. Why, it's your stream," she said.

He stayed, but he paid far more attention to Mrs. Dangerfield than to the fishing. Besides her charming eyes and delightful voice, her air of fragility made a strong appeal to his vigorous robustness. His first discomfort sternly vanquished, its place was taken by the keenest desire to remain in her presence. He not only stayed with them till the Twins had caught their three fish, but he walked nearly to Colet House with them, and at last bade them good-by with an air of the deepest reluctance. It can hardly be doubted that he had been smitten by an emotional lightning-stroke, as the French put it, or, as we more gently phrase it, that he had fallen in love at first sight.

As he walked back to the Grange he was regretting that he had not received the social advances of his neighbors with greater warmth. If, instead of staying firmly at home, he had been moving about among them, he would have met Mrs. Dangerfield earlier and by now be in a fortunate condition of meeting her often. It did not for a moment enter his mind that if he had met her stiffly in a drawing-room he might easily have failed to fall in love with her at all. He cudgeled his brains to find some way of meeting her again and meeting her often. He was to meet her quite soon without any effort on his part.

It is possible that Mrs. Dangerfield had observed that Sir James had been smitten by that emotional *coup de foudre*, for she was walking with a much brisker step and there was a warmer color in her cheeks.

After he had bidden them good-by and had turned back to

Edgar Jepson

the Grange, she said in a really cheerful tone:

"I expect Sir James finds it rather dull at the Grange after the exciting life he had in Africa."

"Rather!", said the Twins with one quickly assenting voice.

She had not missed Sir James' sentence about the superiority of Erebus' blackmailing to her fishing. But she knew the Twins far too well to ask them for an explanation of it before him. None the less it clung to her mind.

At supper therefore she said: "What did Sir James mean by calling you a blackmailer, Erebus?"

The Terror knew from her tone that she was resolved to have the explanation; and he said suavely:

"Oh, it was about the fishing."

"How—about the fishing?" said Mrs. Dangerfield quickly.

"Well, he didn't want to give us leave. In fact he never answered our letter asking for it," said the Terror.

"And of course we couldn't stand that; and we had to make him," said Erebus sternly.

"Make him? How did you make him?" said Mrs. Dangerfield.

The Terror told her.

Mrs. Dangerfield looked surprised and annoyed, but much less surprised and annoyed than the ordinary mother would have looked on learning that her offspring had blackmailed a complete stranger. She felt chiefly annoyed by the fact that the complete stranger they had chosen to blackmail should be Sir James.

"Then you did blackmail him," she said in a tone of dismay.

"He seemed to think that we were—like the Douglases used to," said the Terror in an amiable tone.

"But surely you knew that blackmailing is very wrong—very wrong, indeed," said Mrs. Dangerfield.

"Well, he *did* seem to think so," said the Terror. "But we thought he was prejudiced; and we didn't take much notice of him."

"And we couldn't possibly let him take no notice of our letter, Mum—it was such a polite letter—and not take it out of him," said Erebus.

"And it hasn't done any harm, you know. We wanted those trout ever so much more than he did," said the Terror.

Mrs. Dangerfield said nothing for a while; and her frown deepened as she pondered how to deal with the affair. She was still chiefly annoyed that Sir James should have been the victim. The Twins gazed at her with a sympathetic gravity which by no means meant that they were burdened by a sense of wrong-doing. They were merely sorry that she was annoyed.

"Well, there's nothing for it: you'll have to apologize to Sir James—both of you," she said at last.

"Apologize to him! But he never answered our letter!" cried Erebus.

The Terror hesitated a moment, opened his mouth to speak, shut it, opened it again and said in a soothing tone: "All right, Mum; we'll apologize."

"I'll take you to the Grange to-morrow afternoon to do it," said Mrs. Dangerfield, for she thought that unless she were present the Twins would surely contrive to repeat the offense in the apology and compel Sir James to invite them to continue to fish.

There had been some such intention in the Terror's mind, for his face fell: an apology in the presence of his mother would have to be a real apology. But he said amiably: "All right; just as you like, Mum."

Erebus scowled very darkly, and muttered fierce things under her breath. After supper, without moving him at all, she reproached the Terror bitterly for not refusing firmly.

The next afternoon therefore the three of them walked, by a foot-path across the fields, to the Grange. Surprise and extreme pleasure were mingled with the respect with which Mawley ushered them into the drawing-room; and he almost ran to apprise Sir James of their coming.

Sir James was at the moment wondering very anxiously whether he would find Mrs. Dangerfield on the bank of the stream that evening watching her children fish. His night's rest had trebled his interest in her and his desire to see more, a great deal more, of her. The appeal to him of her frail and delicate beauty was stronger than ever.

At dinner the night before he had questioned Mawley, with a careless enough air, about her, and had learned that Mr. Dangerfield had been dead seven years, that she had a very small income, and was hard put to it to make both ends meet.

His compassion had been deeply stirred; she was so plainly a creature who deserved the smoothest path in life. He wished that he could now, at once, see his way to help her to that smoothest path; and he was resolved to find that way as soon as he possibly could.

When Mawley told him that she was in his drawing-room, he could scarcely believe his joyful ears. He had to put a constraint on himself to walk to its door in a decorous fashion fit for Mawley's eyes, and not dash to it at full speed. He entered the room with his eyes shining very brightly.

Mrs. Dangerfield greeted him coldly, even a little haughtily. She was looking grave and ill at ease.

"I've come about a rather unpleasant matter, Sir James," she said as they shook hands. "I find that these children have been blackmailing you; and I've brought them to apologize. I—I'm exceedingly distressed about it."

"Oh, there's no need to be—no need at all. It was rather a joke," Sir James protested quickly.

"But blackmailing isn't a joke—though of course they didn't realize what a serious thing it is—"

"It was the Douglases doing it," broke in the Terror in an explanatory tone.

"I don't think you ought to have given way to them, Sir James," said Mrs. Dangerfield severely.

"But I hadn't any choice, I assure you. They had me in a cleft stick," protested Sir James.

"Well then you ought to have come straight to me," said

Mrs. Dangerfield.

"Oh, but really—a little fishing—what is a little fishing? I couldn't come bothering you about a thing like that," protested Sir James.

"But it isn't a little thing if you get it like that," said Mrs. Dangerfield. "Anyhow, it's going to stop; and they're going to apologize."

She turned to them; and as if at a signal the Twins said with one voice:

"I apologize for blackmailing you, Sir James."

The Terror spoke with an amiable nonchalance; the words came very stiffly from the lips of Erebus, and she wore a lowering air.

"Oh, not at all—not at all—don't mention it. Besides, I owe you an apology for not answering your letter," said Sir James in all the discomfort of a man receiving something that is not his due. Then he heaved a sigh of relief and added: "Well, that's all right. And now I hope you'll do all the fishing you want to."

"Certainly not; I can't allow them to fish your water any more," said Mrs. Dangerfield sternly.

"Oh, but really," said Sir James with a harried air.

"No," said Mrs. Dangerfield; and she held out her hand.

"But you'll have some tea—after that hot walk!" cried Sir James.

"No, thank you, I must be getting home," said Mrs. Dangerfield firmly.

Sir James did not press her to stay; he saw that her mind was made up.

He opened the door of the drawing-room, and they filed out. As Erebus passed out, she turned and made a hideous grimace at him. She was desirous that he should not overrate her apology.

Edgar Jepson

CHAPTER XIV

AND THE SOUND OF WEDDING BELLS

Sir James came through the hall with them, carelessly taking his cap from the horn of an antelope on the wall as he passed it. He came down the steps, along the gardens to the side gate, and through it into the park, talking to Mrs. Dangerfield of the changes he had found in the gardens of the Grange after his last five years of big game shooting about the world.

Mrs. Dangerfield had not liked her errand; and she was in no mood for companionship. But she could not drive him from her side on his own land. They walked slowly; the Twins forged ahead. When Sir James and Mrs. Dangerfield came out of the park, the Twins were out of sight. Mere politeness demanded that he should walk the rest of the way with her.

When the Twins were out of the hearing of their mother and Sir James, the Terror said:

"Well, he was quite decent about it. It made him much more uncomfortable than we were. I suppose it was because we're more used to Mum."

"What did the silly idiot want to give us away at all for?" said the unappeased Erebus.

"Oh, well; he didn't mean to. It was an accident, you know," said the Terror.

His provident mind foresaw advantages to be attained from a closer intimacy with Sir James.

"Accident! People shouldn't have accidents like that!" said Erebus in a tone of bitter scorn.

When he and Mrs. Dangerfield came out of the park, Sir James diplomatically fell to lauding the Twins to the skies, their beauty, their grace and their intelligence. The diplomacy was not natural (he was no diplomat) but accidental: the Twins were the only subject he could at the moment think of. He could not have found a quicker way to Mrs. Dangerfield's approval. She had been disposed to dislike him for having been blackmailed by them; his praise of them softened her heart. Discussing them, they came right to the gate of Colet House; and it was only natural that she should invite him to tea. He accepted with alacrity. At tea he changed the subject: they talked about her.

He came home yet more interested in her, resolved yet more firmly to see more of her. With a natural simplicity he used his skill in woodcraft to compass his end, and availed himself of the covert afforded by the common to watch Colet House. Thanks to this simple device he was able to meet or overtake Mrs. Dangerfield, somewhere in the first half-mile of her afternoon walk.

They grew intimate quickly, thanks chiefly to his simple directness; and he found that his first impression that he wanted her more than he had ever wanted anything in his life, more even than he had wanted, in his enthusiastic youth, to shoot a black rhinoceros, was right. He had been making arrangements for another shooting expedition; but he perceived now very clearly, indeed, that it was his immediate duty to settle down in life, provide the Hall with a mistress, and do his duty by his estate and his neighbors.

He had had no experience of women; but his hunting had developed his instinct and he perceived that he must proceed very warily indeed, that to bring Mrs. Dangerfield over the boundary-line of friendship into the land of romance was the most difficult enterprise he had ever dreamed of. But he had a stout heart, the hunter's pertinacity, and a burning resolve to succeed.

He wanted all the help he could get; and he saw that the Twins would be useful friends in the matter. But did they chance on him walking with their mother, or at tea with her, they held politely but gloomily aloof. He must abate their hostility.

He contrived, therefore, to meet them on the common as they were starting one afternoon on an expedition, greeted them cheerfully, stopped and said: "I'm awfully sorry I gave you away the other day. But I never saw your mother till I'd done it."

"Don't mention it," said the Terror with cold graciousness.

"So you ought to be," said Erebus.

"It's a pity you should lose your fishing. If I'd known how good you both were at it, I should have given you leave when I got your letter," said Sir James hypocritically. "But I was misinformed about you."

"It's worse that mother should lose the trout. She does hate butcher's meat so, and it is so difficult to get her to eat properly," said Erebus in a somewhat mollified tone.

"It's like that, is it?" said Sir James quickly; and an expression of deep concern filled his face.

"Yes, and she did eat those trout," said Erebus plaintively.

Sir James knitted his brow in frowning thought; and the Twins watched him with little hope in their faces. Of a sudden his brow grew smooth; and he said:

"Look here: you mayn't fish my water; but there's no reason why you shouldn't fish Glazebrook's. *I* think that a man who nets his water loses all rights."

"Yes, he does," said the Terror firmly.

"Well, with one watching while the other fishes, it ought to be safe enough; and I'll stand the racket if you get prosecuted and fined. I want to take it out of that fellow Glazebrook— he's not a sportsman."

The Terror's face had brightened; but he said: "But how should we account for the fish we took home?"

"You can reckon them presents from me. They would be— practically—if I'm going to pay the fines," said Sir James.

The eyes of both the Twins danced: this was a fashion of dealing tenderly with exactitude which appealed to them. The Terror himself could not have been more tender with it.

"That's a ripping idea!" said Erebus in a tone of the warmest approval.

The peace was thus concluded.

Having thus abated their hostility, Sir James spared no pains

Edgar Jepson

to win their good will. He gave the Terror a rook-rifle and Erebus boxes of chocolate. If he chanced on them when motoring in the afternoon he would carry them off, bicycles and all, in his car and regale them with sumptuous teas at the Grange; and at Colet House he entertained them with stories of the African forest which thrilled Mrs. Dangerfield even more than they thrilled them. But he won their hearts most by his sympathy with them in the matter of their mother's appetite, and by joining them in little plots to obtain delicacies for her.

Having discovered how grateful it was to her, he lost no opportunity of taking the short cut to her heart by praising them. He laid himself out to be useful to her, to entertain and amuse her, trying to make for himself as large as possible a place in her life. She was not long discovering that he was in love with her; and the discovery came as a very pleasant shock. None of the neighbors, much less Captain Baster, who, during her stay at Colet House, had asked her to marry them, had attracted her so strongly as did Sir James. Even as her delicacy made the strongest appeal to his vigorous robustness, so his vigorous robustness made the strongest appeal to her delicacy.

But Little Deeping is a censorious place; and its gossips are the keener for having so few chances of plying their active tongues. When no less than four ladies had on four several occasions met Sir James and Mrs. Dangerfield walking together along the lanes, those tongues began to wag.

Then old Mrs. Blenkinsop, the childless widow of a Common Councilman of London, one morning met the Twins in the village. They greeted her politely and made to escape. But she was in the mood, her most constant mood, to babble. She stopped them, and with a knowing air, and even more offensive smile, said:

"So, young people, we're going to hear the sound of wedding bells very soon in Little Deeping, are we?"

Erebus merely scowled at her, for more than once she had talked about them; but the Terror, in a tone of somewhat perfunctory politeness, said:

"Are we?"

"I should have thought you would have known all about it," she said with a cackling little giggle. "Mind you tell me as soon as you're told: I want to be one of the first to congratulate your dear mother."

"What do you mean?" snapped the Terror with a disconcerting suddenness; and his eyes shone very bright and threatening in a steady glare into her own.

"Oh, nothing—nothing!" cried Mrs. Blenkinsop, flustered by his sternness. "Only seeing Sir James so much with your mother—But there—there's probably nothing in it—the Morgans always were rovers—one foot at sea and one on shore—I dare say he'll be in the middle of Africa before the week is out. Good morning—good morning."

With that she sprang, more lightly than she had sprung for years, into the grocer's shop.

The Twins looked after her with uneasy eyes, frowning. Then Erebus said: "Silly old idiot!"

The Terror said nothing; he walked on frowning. At last he broke out: "This won't do! We can't have these old idiots gossiping about Mum. And it's a beastly nuisance: Sir James was making things so much more cheerful for her."

"But you don't think there's anything in what the old cat said? It would be perfectly horrid to have a stepfather!" cried Erebus in a panic.

The Terror walked on, frowning in deep thought.

"*Do* you think there's anything in it?" cried Erebus.

"I dare say there is. Sir James is always about with Mum; and he's always very civil to us—people aren't generally," said the Terror.

"Oh, but we must stop it! We must stop it at once!" cried Erebus.

"Why must we?"

"It would be perfectly beastly having a step-father, I tell you!" cried Erebus fiercely.

"It isn't altogether what we like—there's Mum," said the Terror. "She does have a rotten time of it—always being hard up and never going anywhere. And, after all, we shouldn't mind Sir James when we got used to him."

"But we should! And look how we stopped the Cruncher!"

"Sir James isn't like the Cruncher—at all," said the Terror.

"All stepfathers are alike; and they're beastly!" cried Erebus.

"Now, it's no good your getting yourself obstinate about it," said the Terror firmly. "That won't be of any use at all, if they've made up their minds. But what's bothering me is what that old cat meant by saying that the Morgans were rovers."

Erebus' frown deepened as she knitted her brow over the cryptic utterance of Mrs. Blenkinsop. Then she said in a tone of considerable relief:

"She must have meant that he wasn't really in earnest about marrying Mum."

"Yes, that's what she did mean," growled the Terror. "And she'll go about telling everybody that he's only fooling."

"But I don't think he is. I don't think he would," said Erebus quickly.

"No more do I," said the Terror.

They walked nearly fifty yards in silence. Then the Terror's face cleared and brightened; and he said cheerfully:

"I know the thing to do! I'll go and ask him his intentions. That's what people said old Hawley ought to have done when the Cut—you know: that fellow from Rowington—was fooling about with Miss Hawley."

"All right, we'll go and ask him," said Erebus with equal cheerfulness.

"No, no, you can't go. I must go alone," said the Terror quickly. "It's the kind of thing the men of the family always do—people said so about Miss Hawley—and I'm the only man of the family about. If Uncle Maurice were in London and not in Vienna, we might send for him to do it."

Erebus burst into bitter complaint. She alleged that the restrictions which were applied to the ordinary girl should by no means be applied to her, since she was not ordinary; that since they cooperated in everything else they ought to

Edgar Jepson

cooperate in this; that he was much more successful in those exploits in which they did cooperate, than in those which he performed alone.

"It's no good talking like that: it isn't the thing to do," said the Terror with very cold severity. "You know what Mrs. Morton said about Miss Hawley and the Cut—that the men of the family did it."

"You're only a boy; and I'm as old as you!" snapped Erebus.

"Well, when there isn't a man to do a thing, a boy does it. So it's no use you're making a fuss," said the Terror in a tone of finality.

Erebus protested that the upshot of his going alone would be that Sir James would presently be their detested stepfather; but he went alone, early in the afternoon.

He was now on such familiar terms at the Grange that Mawley took him straight to the smoking-room, where his master was smoking a cigar over his after-lunch coffee. Sir James welcomed him warmly, for he was beginning to learn that the Terror was quite good company, in the country, and poured him out a cup of coffee.

The Terror put sugar and cream into it and forthwith, since a simple matter of this kind did not seem to him to call for the exercise of his usual diplomacy, said with firm directness: "I've come to ask your intentions, sir."

"My intentions?" said Sir James, not taking him.

"Yes. You see some of the old cats who live about here are saying that you're only fooling," said the Terror.

"The deuce they are!" cried Sir James sharply with a sudden and angry comprehension.

"Yes. So of course the thing to do was to ask your intentions," said the Terror firmly.

"Of course—of course," said Sir James.

He looked at the Terror; and in spite of his anger his eyes twinkled. Then he added gravely: "My intentions are not only extremely serious but they're extremely immediate. I'd marry your mother to-morrow if she'd let me."

"That's all right," said the Terror with a faint sigh of relief. "Of course I knew you were all right. Only, it was the thing to do, with these silly old idiots talking."

"Quite so—quite so," said Sir James.

There was a pause; and Sir James looked again at the Terror tranquilly drinking his coffee, in a somewhat appealing fashion, for he had been suffering badly from all the doubts and fears of the lover; and the Terror's serenity was soothing.

Then with a sudden craving for comfort and reassurance, he said: "Do you think your mother would marry me?"

"I haven't the slightest idea; women are so funny," said the Terror with a sage air.

Sir James pulled at his mustache. Then the compulsion to have some one's opinion of his chances, even if it was only a small boy's, came on him strongly; and he said:

"I wish I knew what to do. As it is we're very good friends; and if I asked her to marry me, I might spoil that."

The Terror considered the point for a minute or two; then he said: "I don't think you would. Mum's very sensible, though she is so pretty."

Sir James frowned deeply in his utter perplexity; then he said: "I'll risk it!"

He rang the bell and ordered his car. He talked to the Terror jerkily and somewhat incoherently till it came; and the Terror observed his perturbation with considerable interest. It seemed to him very curious in a hard-bitten hunter of big game. They started and in the two level miles to Little Deeping Sir James changed his car's speeds nine times.

As they came very slowly up to Colet House, the Terror said with an air of detachment: "I should think, you know, Mum could be rushed."

He had definitely made up his mind that it would be a good thing for her.

"If I only could!" said Sir James in a tone of feverish doubt.

Mrs. Dangerfield was mending a rent in a frock of Erebus when he entered the drawing-room; and at the first glance she knew, with a thrill half of pleasure, half of apprehension, why he had come.

At the sight of her Sir James felt his tremulous courage oozing out of him; but with what was left of it he blurted out desperately:

"Look here, Anne, dear, I want you to marry me!"

"Oh!" said Mrs. Dangerfield, rising quickly.

"Yes, I want it more than ever I wanted anything in my life!"

Mrs. Dangerfield's face was one flush; and she cried: "B-b-but it's out of the question. I—I'm old enough to be your mother!"

"Now how?—I'm three years and seven months older than you," said Sir James, taken aback.

"I shall be an old woman while you're still quite young!" she protested.

"You won't ever be old! You're not the kind!" cried Sir James with some heat; and then with sudden understanding: "If that's your only reason, why, that settles it!"

With that he picked her up and kissed her four times.

When he set her down and held her at arm's length, gazing at her with devouring eyes, she gasped somewhat faintly: "Oh, James, you are—ever so much more—impetuous—than I thought. You gave me—no time."

"Thank goodness, I took the Terror's tip!" said Sir James.

Edgar Jepson

Choose from Thousands of 1stWorldLibrary Classics By

A. M. Barnard
Ada Leverson
Adolphus William Ward
Aesop
Agatha Christie
Alexander Aaronsohn
Alexander Kielland
Alexandre Dumas
Alfred Gatty
Alfred Ollivant
Alice Duer Miller
Alice Turner Curtis
Alice Dunbar
Allen Chapman
Alleyne Ireland
Ambrose Bierce
Amelia E. Barr
Amory H. Bradford
Andrew Lang
Andrew McFarland Davis
Andy Adams
Angela Brazil
Anna Alice Chapin
Anna Sewell
Annie Besant
Annie Hamilton Donnell
Annie Payson Call
Annie Roe Carr
Annonaymous
Anton Chekhov
Archibald Lee Fletcher
Arnold Bennett
Arthur C. Benson
Arthur Conan Doyle
Arthur M. Winfield
Arthur Ransome
Arthur Schnitzler
Arthur Train
Atticus
B.H. Baden-Powell
B. M. Bower
B. C. Chatterjee
Baroness Emmuska Orczy
Baroness Orczy
Basil King
Bayard Taylor
Ben Macomber
Bertha Muzzy Bower
Bjornstjerne Bjornson

Booth Tarkington
Boyd Cable
Bram Stoker
C. Collodi
C. E. Orr
C. M. Ingleby
Carolyn Wells
Catherine Parr Traill
Charles A. Eastman
Charles Amory Beach
Charles Dickens
Charles Dudley Warner
Charles Farrar Browne
Charles Ives
Charles Kingsley
Charles Klein
Charles Hanson Towne
Charles Lathrop Pack
Charles Romyn Dake
Charles Whibley
Charles Willing Beale
Charlotte M. Braeme
Charlotte M. Yonge
Charlotte Perkins Stetson
Clair W. Hayes
Clarence Day Jr.
Clarence E. Mulford
Clemence Housman
Confucius
Coningsby Dawson
Cornelis DeWitt Wilcox
Cyril Burleigh
D. H. Lawrence
Daniel Defoe
David Garnett
Dinah Craik
Don Carlos Janes
Donald Keyhoe
Dorothy Kilner
Dougan Clark
Douglas Fairbanks
E. Nesbit
E. P. Roe
E. Phillips Oppenheim
E. S. Brooks
Earl Barnes
Edgar Rice Burroughs
Edith Van Dyne
Edith Wharton

Edward Everett Hale
Edward J. O'Biren
Edward S. Ellis
Edwin L. Arnold
Eleanor Atkins
Eleanor Hallowell Abbott
Eliot Gregory
Elizabeth Gaskell
Elizabeth McCracken
Elizabeth Von Arnim
Ellem Key
Emerson Hough
Emilie F. Carlen
Emily Bronte
Emily Dickinson
Enid Bagnold
Enilor Macartney Lane
Erasmus W. Jones
Ernie Howard Pie
Ethel May Dell
Ethel Turner
Ethel Watts Mumford
Eugene Sue
Eugenie Foa
Eugene Wood
Eustace Hale Ball
Evelyn Everett-green
Everard Cotes
F. H. Cheley
F. J. Cross
F. Marion Crawford
Fannie E. Newberry
Federick Austin Ogg
Ferdinand Ossendowski
Fergus Hume
Florence A. Kilpatrick
Fremont B. Deering
Francis Bacon
Francis Darwin
Frances Hodgson Burnett
Frances Parkinson Keyes
Frank Gee Patchin
Frank Harris
Frank Jewett Mather
Frank L. Packard
Frank V. Webster
Frederic Stewart Isham
Frederick Trevor Hill
Frederick Winslow Taylor

Friedrich Kerst
Friedrich Nietzsche
Fyodor Dostoyevsky
G.A. Henty
G.K. Chesterton
Gabrielle E. Jackson
Garrett P. Serviss
Gaston Leroux
George A. Warren
George Ade
Geroge Bernard Shaw
George Cary Eggleston
George Durston
George Ebers
George Eliot
George Gissing
George MacDonald
George Meredith
George Orwell
George Sylvester Viereck
George Tucker
George W. Cable
George Wharton James
Gertrude Atherton
Gordon Casserly
Grace E. King
Grace Gallatin
Grace Greenwood
Grant Allen
Guillermo A. Sherwell
Gulielma Zollinger
Gustav Flaubert
H. A. Cody
H. B. Irving
H.C. Bailey
H. G. Wells
H. H. Munro
H. Irving Hancock
H. R. Naylor
H. Rider Haggard
H. W. C. Davis
Haldeman Julius
Hall Caine
Hamilton Wright Mabie
Hans Christian Andersen
Harold Avery
Harold McGrath
Harriet Beecher Stowe
Harry Castlemon
Harry Coghill
Harry Houidini

Hayden Carruth
Helent Hunt Jackson
Helen Nicolay
Hendrik Conscience
Hendy David Thoreau
Henri Barbusse
Henrik Ibsen
Henry Adams
Henry Ford
Henry Frost
Henry James
Henry Jones Ford
Henry Seton Merriman
Henry W Longfellow
Herbert A. Giles
Herbert Carter
Herbert N. Casson
Herman Hesse
Hildegard G. Frey
Homer
Honore De Balzac
Horace B. Day
Horace Walpole
Horatio Alger Jr.
Howard Pyle
Howard R. Garis
Hugh Lofting
Hugh Walpole
Humphry Ward
Ian Maclaren
Inez Haynes Gillmore
Irving Bacheller
Isabel Cecilia Williams
Isabel Hornibrook
Israel Abrahams
Ivan Turgenev
J.G.Austin
J. Henri Fabre
J. M. Barrie
J. M. Walsh
J. Macdonald Oxley
J. R. Miller
J. S. Fletcher
J. S. Knowles
J. Storer Clouston
J. W. Duffield
Jack London
Jacob Abbott
James Allen
James Andrews
James Baldwin

James Branch Cabell
James DeMille
James Joyce
James Lane Allen
James Lane Allen
James Oliver Curwood
James Oppenheim
James Otis
James R. Driscoll
Jane Abbott
Jane Austen
Jane L. Stewart
Janet Aldridge
Jens Peter Jacobsen
Jerome K. Jerome
Jessie Graham Flower
John Buchan
John Burroughs
John Cournos
John F. Kennedy
John Gay
John Glasworthy
John Habberton
John Joy Bell
John Kendrick Bangs
John Milton
John Philip Sousa
John Taintor Foote
Jonas Lauritz Idemil Lie
Jonathan Swift
Joseph A. Altsheler
Joseph Carey
Joseph Conrad
Joseph E. Badger Jr
Joseph Hergesheimer
Joseph Jacobs
Jules Vernes
Julian Hawthrone
Julie A Lippmann
Justin Huntly McCarthy
Kakuzo Okakura
Karle Wilson Baker
Kate Chopin
Kenneth Grahame
Kenneth McGaffey
Kate Langley Bosher
Kate Langley Bosher
Katherine Cecil Thurston
Katherine Stokes
L. A. Abbot
L. T. Meade

L. Frank Baum
Latta Griswold
Laura Dent Crane
Laura Lee Hope
Laurence Housman
Lawrence Beasley
Leo Tolstoy
Leonid Andreyev
Lewis Carroll
Lewis Sperry Chafer
Lilian Bell
Lloyd Osbourne
Louis Hughes
Louis Joseph Vance
Louis Tracy
Louisa May Alcott
Lucy Fitch Perkins
Lucy Maud Montgomery
Luther Benson
Lydia Miller Middleton
Lyndon Orr
M. Corvus
M. H. Adams
Margaret E. Sangster
Margret Howth
Margaret Vandercook
Margaret W. Hungerford
Margret Penrose
Maria Edgeworth
Maria Thompson Daviess
Mariano Azuela
Marion Polk Angellotti
Mark Overton
Mark Twain
Mary Austin
Mary Catherine Crowley
Mary Cole
Mary Hastings Bradley
Mary Roberts Rinehart
Mary Rowlandson
M. Wollstonecraft Shelley
Maud Lindsay
Max Beerbohm
Myra Kelly
Nathaniel Hawthrone
Nicolo Machiavelli
O. F. Walton
Oscar Wilde

Owen Johnson
P.G. Wodehouse
Paul and Mabel Thorne
Paul G. Tomlinson
Paul Severing
Percy Brebner
Percy Keese Fitzhugh
Peter B. Kyne
Plato
Quincy Allen
R. Derby Holmes
R. L. Stevenson
R. S. Ball
Rabindranath Tagore
Rahul Alvares
Ralph Bonehill
Ralph Henry Barbour
Ralph Victor
Ralph Waldo Emmerson
Rene Descartes
Ray Cummings
Rex Beach
Rex E. Beach
Richard Harding Davis
Richard Jefferies
Richard Le Gallienne
Robert Barr
Robert Frost
Robert Gordon Anderson
Robert L. Drake
Robert Lansing
Robert Lynd
Robert Michael Ballantyne
Robert W. Chambers
Rosa Nouchette Carey
Rudyard Kipling
Saint Augustine
Samuel B. Allison
Samuel Hopkins Adams
Sarah Bernhardt
Sarah C. Hallowell
Selma Lagerlof
Sherwood Anderson
Sigmund Freud
Standish O'Grady
Stanley Weyman
Stella Benson
Stella M. Francis

Stephen Crane
Stewart Edward White
Stijn Streuvels
Swami Abhedananda
Swami Parmananda
T. S. Ackland
T. S. Arthur
The Princess Der Ling
Thomas A. Janvier
Thomas A Kempis
Thomas Anderton
Thomas Bailey Aldrich
Thomas Bulfinch
Thomas De Quincey
Thomas Dixon
Thomas H. Huxley
Thomas Hardy
Thomas More
Thornton W. Burgess
U. S. Grant
Upton Sinclair
Valentine Williams
Various Authors
Vaughan Kester
Victor Appleton
Victor G. Durham
Victoria Cross
Virginia Woolf
Wadsworth Camp
Walter Camp
Walter Scott
Washington Irving
Wilbur Lawton
Wilkie Collins
Willa Cather
Willard F. Baker
William Dean Howells
William le Queux
W. Makepeace Thackeray
William W. Walter
William Shakespeare
Winston Churchill
Yei Theodora Ozaki
Yogi Ramacharaka
Young E. Allison
Zane Grey